Out of My M

Gaurav

Table of Contents

Acknowledgement

Writing a book is harder than I thought but also more rewarding than I could have ever imagined. None of this would have been possible without the support of many incredible people around me. Firstly, I would thank my mother and father who raised me with love and compassion. I thank my brother deeply for being my friend and support since childhood. A special thanks to my close friends in the UK, who have supported me in every aspect over the last ten years of my lfe. I also want to thanks my wider family, childhood friends and work colleagues as everyone around me has impacted my life experiences in some way or the other and will always remain connected to me.

A special thanks to my publishing team as it would have not been possible to complete this book without your guidance, support and encouragement.

About the Author

Gaurav was born in a small town in India during the mid-80s in a lower middle-class family with very limited resources, however, it was a reasonably stable and happy family.

Since childhood, he had always wondered what this life, or in other words, living, was all about. He used to think why live, if one day you will not be here living anymore. It sometimes felt useless to him. However, for obvious reasons he could not ask this question as everybody seemed to be very comfortable with their lives and from where he was standing, looked like they had every idea what life was about. He could not shake this question away, no matter how much he tried, but slowly, he got busy in school, friends, studies, and eventually stopped thinking about it.

Life took a sudden turn for him when he travelled to the UK and saw a different side of living there which challenged all his assumptions and ideas.

A Trip to Remember the Past

Gaurav was walking out of the Piccadilly Line train station at Heathrow Airport, heading towards the British Airways Lounge. It was a very busy day at work, and he came to the airport straight and still frantically checking his work emails to ensure everything was completed as he was going on a holiday with friends for two and a half weeks. At the same time, at the back of his mind, he knew that he was heading on a holiday, which was going to be an amazing experience. They were heading to Hong Kong then from there would travel to three cities in Japan, including Tokyo, and the trip included attending the Formula 1 Japanese Grand Prix and the 2019 Rugby World cup semi-final in Tokyo. The trip was even more exciting for him as he had always thought of going to Japan and was fascinated by Japanese culture, the success that Japan has had as a country socially and economically in the last fifty years is simply amazing, and a lot is down to their way of living which is different to what they are used to in Western societies. He was just expecting to see a different world. He was flying to Hong Kong with his friend Martin and his wife Anna, who were waiting for him at the BA lounge at Heathrow. Once he had his ticket, he made his way to meet them as he just wanted to get away from the rush at that time and relax. They were going to meet Richard and his wife, Noriko, in Hong

Kong and, after a day, head to Osaka in Japan. From Osaka, they would travel to Hiroshima then Tokyo. From Tokyo, they would return back to Hong Kong, spend a few days there and then back to London. They were all really excited as they knew that it was going to be an amazing trip.

As the plane takes off and now the seat belt signs are off, he relaxes for a moment and goes over the things that need to sort out in his mind. Although he is excited about the trip, he knows that a few work things need to be sorted, which he needs to ensure are completed, even more acutely aware that he has big financial dues coming up, and he is extremely tight with funds at that moment. He had been going through a difficult period financially due to an accumulation of high costs with maintenance at home. This was all pre-planned and booked six months back, so he decided that with all the ongoing financial issues, he would go ahead with the trip and somehow manage the expenses. The last six months for him have been very indifferent, work has kept him busy, but he has been having a very empty feeling, this was not loneliness. He has been ignoring this by keeping himself busy with friends, work and family, but recently he has been having this feeling of there being something more to life than what people usually call living a normal life, but he was not able to understand what it was. He was very confused but convinced that there was something more to life than the limited targets he had set himself to do. Every point in his adult life when he had some success, he thought that was it! But his goals keep moving and what he thought was a success was very relative, only in comparison to someone around him. He wanted to spend some time contemplating this on the holiday as he would so easily get distracted in day-to-day life.

They arrived in Hong Kong the next morning after a long thirteen hours flight, he had been to Hong Kong before and love the city. It's a very vibrant and one of the most cosmopolitan cities in Asia. Their hotel was right in the centre of the city, right next to a huge shopping mall, bars and restaurants. They met Richard and Noriko along with another friend of theirs, Ken, who is a local in Hong Kong and used to work with all of them in London between 2010-2015. It was absolutely great to meet everyone for dinner after three years. They went to a dumplings place downtown in Hong Kong, as Gaurav knew how much Richard loves his food, he had no doubt that the food would be amazing. The last restaurant they probably went to together in London was probably a dumplings place, so this was a great choice. The dumplings with sake was a great start to the trip. By now, he had forgotten all about the things that he needed to worry about and to enjoy the re union with some of his close friends. They were all flying to Osaka the next afternoon, where they would spend a couple of days.

As they started their descent into Osaka, he could already see how beautiful Japan was. Osaka was very close to the ocean, and as the plane started descending and it was close to landing, you could see an incredible view of the city. First impressions of the city were really amazing. A very organised, modern city. Definitely not as big as Tokyo, but still big in its own right. With its own history, and at the same time, exquisitely clean and well planned. Gaurav was simply amazed how organised everything was in Japan, and that was kind of my first impression of Japan, which is what he had in his mind before going to Japan, and it did not disappoint. They checked into their hotels, and then went out for some drinks and dinner that night, a very classic Japanese style restaurant, but equally modern as well. The next day they had Formula 1, so they left early in the morning because it was a bit further away from Osaka. Formula 1, again, unique and great experience. Gaurav has been to Formula 1 racing before, so it was thoroughly enjoyable. There were about 70,000 people there, so a massive crowd and another brilliant day in Japan. The following day after Formula 1, they had a slightly different it was not as exciting as Formula 1, but they were supposed to go out for lunch to this in a fish market. And then after that, they were supposed to go to a few temples and visit some tourist places. The lunch was great, but that day the one thing that sticks to Gaurav very clearly was the visit to the temple, including the walk, as everything reminded him of the rich tradition and history of Japan. As they walked through the street to go into this temple, it was really quite a surreal place. Everything around was very organised and had a sense of harmony which resulted in almost pin-drop silence in most places apart from maybe the area which had small local gift shops and small restaurants.

They spent a couple of days in Osaka and the next stop was Hiroshima. They were about to travel in the bullet train from Osaka to Hiroshima and then from Hiroshima to Tokyo a couple of days later. He was very fond of trains growing up and the bullet train journey was one of highlights of the trip as it was something he wanted to do since he was very young. It was an incredible experience to travel on train with such high speeds. Hiroshima, another beautiful city, not as busy as Osaka but has it has its own importance in history of this world. It was very humbling feeling to go to the atomic bombing site and also see the museum. Till that day Gaurav did not realise that how unaware he was of the war and the events that took place in Hiroshima. But that was a great reminder of what history was what the history of the city was. After spending a couple of days in Hiroshima, we were off to Tokyo.

Again, he was all excited that morning as we were leaving for Tokyo on the bullet train. They came out of the train station and took a taxi to the hotel in Tokyo. Richard and Gaurav got on one taxi with luggage, Martin, Anna and Noriko got on the bigger taxi. As they arrive at the hotel car park, Gaurav reaches for his wallet and realises that he doesn't have it in his pockets. He looks for it in his bag, on the seats but can't find it anywhere. He suddenly realised that he may have forgotten his wallet on the train. He remembered putting it in the pocket in front of the seat, but clearly, he was so excited to be on the train that he forgot his wallet. Richard paid the cab and then they went to the reception. He was in shock for a couple of minutes as he was in a different city on a holiday and losing his wallet would have been was one of the worst things that could happen because he would lose his cards and would have to call the bank to cancel his cards to avoid any fraud. He would also have to ask his friends for help as they would have to pay on his behalf. He was dreading the situation but for some reason within a few minutes of this, he just felt like nothing had happened, almost as if he was forcing himself to feel bad and guilty, but after the initial shock he felt calm which surprised him. His friends also noticed this and one of them mentioned that he was being extremely calm about the situation for someone who's just lost his wallet and all his cards in a foreign country while on holiday. Gaurav had been feeling indifferent for a few months before coming on to this trip.

They had a great first couple of days in Tokyo. The Rugby World Cup game was the next evening. So Gaurav made some arrangements with his friends to ensure that he could have some cash in his hand for the for the rest of the trip because there was no way he could have got a new bank card in Tokyo. Noriko was quick to submit a request to lost and found at the Tokyo train station. Knowing how well organised things were in Japan in general, Gaurav was hopeful to get back his wallet. After a couple of days in Tokyo when they were leaving a theatre where they saw a local a play, Noriko received a message from the Tokyo station lost and found that they found his wallet and he can come and collect it from the station. As soon as Gaurav heard that, he was not that surprised that he'd got his wallet but he was ecstatic that he got his wallet back because although the cards were cancelled, at least he knew that he had his wallet back with him and there were a few other things in the wallet which was still useful to him. This incident made his trip even more memorable given lows and then the highs of the trip. Similar to Osaka and Hiroshima, they visited a number of tourist places in Tokyo. One thing that stood out for him in Tokyo as well was one of the temples in the city but on top of a hill.

As they walked towards the main temple on the narrow uphill roads with tall trees and several other small temples around, they spent a little bit of time there. While some of

Gaurav's friends were in the gift shop after the tour of the temple, Gaurav was just walking around outside in the garden. There was a small structure with an inclined roof in the corner of the garden, which reminded him of something he had seen in the past, but he could not recall what it was. And suddenly, as he looked at the temple, it just incredibly brought back thought to his mind which was related to the death of his grandfather as it looked the same as burial ghat where his body was burnt when he died. This is where Gaurav's grandfather passed away, and the rituals were done after his death. And this temple and its surroundings in Japan literally, for some reason, provoked that memory in his head. And it was not just memory like a usual memory as in passing by thought. But it was very real. It was as if Gaurav was literally there in his hometown as a young boy, and looking at that temple on an early morning, the day his grandfather passed away. It was a very unique memory in a way because it felt very real at that time. It was almost as if Gaurav was in both places at the same time. That's how the strong memory was, and it was not like passing by memory. He just thought to himself, *Oh, that was a very unique memory of my grandfather, which I rarely recalled in the last decade.* That day, he could not shake off the memories of his grandfather, and he kept thinking about him throughout the rest of the day. As he lay on his bed that night rather than thinking about the day in Tokyo, Gaurav just slipped into the memory of his grandfather's last day.

When he was around ten years old, one evening, he was at his cousin's house, and a number of them were playing hide and seek. Suddenly one of his uncles started shouting his name, he thought this was just to get him out of hiding so that he was out of the game. he continued to hide, till they sounded very serious and he could see that all others playing had come out as well. His uncle angrily asked him to get ready to go home, and he wasn't ready to go home until he said that his grandfather was not very well and he should go home immediately to meet him. On his way home, Gaurav was still annoyed that he had to stop playing and leave. As he reached home, he noticed that there were around ten people standing outside his house, which was unusual late in the evening. As he walked into the house, he saw a couple of sad faces on the way and was already worried that his grandfather was not very well. As he walked in, he saw him laying very peacefully on his bed and Gaurav's mother in tears. He immediately knew that he had passed away.

Gaurav was not sure how to feel at that time. He did not cry but felt very sad and quietly sat down in one corner of the room. His mother angrily said to him that because he was too keen to go and play with his cousins that he missed seeing his grandfather alive the last time who was asking about him. Gaurav was not sure what to feel as he was still annoyed from having to come back and then find out that his grandfather has passed away. His body was taken on a van with an open back to the cremation ground within a couple of hours of his death. Gaurav rode with his body at the back of the van with his uncles and sat next to it all the way to the cremation ground. His father and a few others had travelled on their bikes and scooters to be there and make the required arrangements before they arrived with the body. As per Hindu tradition, the body is always burnt, and usually, the place for cremation is called burial or burning ghats and mostly located at the bank of a river. It was the same in his town. The burial ghat was located at the bank of river Brahmani, which was in a full rage that night. Gaurav arrived there at about 4 am in the morning when the rituals were going to begin before the body could be burnt. This was all a new experience for him. He had heard of this process before but had never been so close. He still did not fully realise what had just happened and what it really meant when someone passed away, so he was almost excited to see what was going on around him. After the rituals were done, his father lit the pyre with a burning log of wood. Gaurav was sitting seventy yards away from the fire as the day was breaking, and the whole surrounding was quiet with the gushing sound of the river. He could see his grandfather's body burn and get all mixed with the burning wood as he watched with one of his uncles standing next to him. He could hear crackling noises, which his uncle pointed out as his bones and joints burned. Gaurav was not terrified but was suddenly shocked about how fragile life is. One moment a person is there, and the next moment, he can go from existence. This is the first time he ever thought about what being alive really meant. The thought faded away by the time he was back home. It was a sad atmosphere in the house. However, everyone was talking well about his grandfather, how he was fair and hardworking and died in a happy way rather than any suffering. Gaurav was extremely tired, so he slept that day, but the next day when he woke up in the morning, he started to think that he would never see his grandfather again. As this feeling just sunk in, he cried for about hours that morning without any trigger.

This sudden memory of his grandfather triggered loads of past memories specially his childhood which he had mostly forgotten about. Throughout this trip, he had remembered many past incidents which made him realise that he had totally forgotten the wonder he used to have about life. In the process of survival in this world, Gaurav had totally forgotten how curious he used to be about life. But now he thinks that he knows everything about life because of which he lost the curiosity and wonder he used to have as a young boy.

Chapter 1: The Early Life

Gaurav was born in Rourkela, a small town in Odisha, India during the mid-80s. The town is surrounded by a range of hills and encircled by rivers Koel, Sankha, and Brahmani. The town is located in areas that were once covered by dense forests, which were once a favourite hunting ground for the kings in the past and was full of wildlife. The place boasted a very tropical climate where it rained more in summers compared to the winters. The town was founded in 1954 and was turned into an industrial town in the early 60s. India's first public sector steel plant facility was established in Rourkela with the help of German businesses Krupp and Demag. In the late 1950s and early 1960s, the town was the largest German colony outside Germany.

Gaurav was the firstborn in his family. He only had a younger brother named Dhruv. His other family members were his father, his mother, and his grandparents. Although his grandmother died when he was quite young, so he did not remember her that much. His father used to tell him about her. She used to call him Chitra, which means a picture because he looked very much like his grandfather. Gaurav's grandmother used to take care of him and help his mother with the household as well. But she died because of a heart attack. The whole colony attended her final rights, as she was a very reputable person. But to Gaurav, she was just like a blurred picture in his mind. The only way for him to learn how his grandmother looked was by a picture, the only of her there was, which hung on one of the walls. It seemed like the picture was clicked on some special occasion.

At that time, in India, the rate of poverty was around 80% per cent. People used to live in small houses, more like a shed, with just one room and a dozen mouths to feed. Affording a luxurious life was difficult to accomplish. People used to take loans from the ones who were wealthy enough, which they had to return with higher interest later on.

If they were not able to return the money on time, these people used to threaten them and even try to hurt their families. With no way to escape or return the money due to insufficient income, poor people committing suicide was a not uncommon.

Gaurav's family belonged to the lower-middle-class category. They used to live in a small house which comprised of a bedroom, living room, a kitchen, and bathroom which was occupied by five people. On the scale of poverty for the time, his family was not that poor, but the income was hand to mouth. His father was the only person who was earning in the house. Both the brothers used to go to a small school in the town. Even with fewer resources available, they were living a happy life. The financial instability was there, but his father never let his children sleep with an empty stomach. He was getting them food, and the household was never empty.

The family used to attend festivals and used to go out on occasion. They celebrated all festivals with their families as in India, you and your relatives are more likely to visit each other on a daily basis if you live close to each other. His mother was a housewife, just like every other married woman in India. The concept of a woman working was not unusual in the family as his mother's sister was a teacher and father's sister used to work in an office, her mother chose to be a housewife, keeping the house under care.

She was responsible for taking care of her children, looking after all the household, cleaning, attending to guests in case they paid a visit. In comparison to this, his father used to work as an engineer in a steel factory. He was in charge of running a blast furnace that used to melt iron. He used to come back from work around midnight after twelve. By that time, Gaurav and Dhruv used to be asleep, so their father never got the chance to spend much time with his children. He did use to take them to school every morning. That is how they spent some father-son time on their way to school.

Since the beginning, Gaurav always had a tsunami of thoughts running in his mind. His thoughts were

3

extraordinary for someone of his age. Where the other kids of his age used to think about playing all day and running from here and there in their shorts, he used to sit or wander around in his surroundings, observing every small detail, from the movement of leaves to a spider knitting its web.

The increase in a child's ability to think and the reason is referred to as cognitive or intellectual development. It has to do with how they arrange their minds, ideas, and thoughts in order to have a better understanding of the world.

It is not like he never played with other kids. He was a very social child. Everybody loved him. But in solitude, he used to wonder and gather wool, ask questions to himself, and hope that one day he will get the answers.

He used to take part in all the activities happening in his town. Whether it was to play Holi (a Hindu occasion) or getting firecrackers for Diwali (another Hindu occasion), he was always spotted with his group of friends.

One day, he asked his mother why they celebrate Holi and Diwali. His mother explained to him that Holi used to be a rite performed by married women for the safety of their families. They used to worship Raka (the full moon) and ask for his blessings. Although, the real meaning of the festival has been altered over time.

It is believed that people have been celebrating Holi since even before Christ. The festival is meant to celebrate the victory of good over evil. According to legend, After Lord Vishnu assassinated the younger brother of the demon, Hiranyakashipu. This enraged the demon kind, and he avenged his brother by killing Lord Vishnu, and forced people to worship him.

But his reign was cut short when nobody but his own son, Prahalad, understood that his father was not a good man and went against his father's orders. This treachery angered the demon king, and he decided to kill his own son with the help of his sister, Holika, who had the ability that kept her safe even in fire.

So, Holika lit up a fire and dragged Prahalad into it. But the tables were turned when Holika was the one to get burned, and Prahalad walked out of the fire safe. After that, he killed his father, and that is why they celebrate Holi, to celebrate the burning of evil into the fire. Prahalad was convinced that God is in everything, every object, every fabric of this world, so when he prayed, God came out of the wall and killed his father. The story was fascinating to Gaurav and also bugged him at the same time as he could never understand how God could be in everything if he was like a human being.

During Diwali, Gaurav's mother explained that they celebrate this festival in memories of lord Rama, his wife Sita and his brother Dhruv's return to their homeland after fourteen years of exile. It is believed that the village itself lit the way for lord Rama, after he defeated the demon Ravana.

This knowledge fascinated Gaurav a lot as he noticed how often the story of Rama and the values presented are used to compare relationships and roles within Indian families. A son should be like Ram. A brother should be like Laxman, a wife and daughter should be like Sita and so on.

One day, Gaurav was playing with his friends. It was the time of twilight. He looked at the sun and watched it set. He kept on looking until the sun set completely and the sky turned black, with stars shimmering above him. His friends asked him what is he looking at. It is just a sunset, like every other day. To which he asked them what do they think is the purpose of this process. He asked about their thoughts on the process of day turning into night and then the night turning into day again, every day. To which they thought that he had been thinking nonsense and left him there. He stayed on the ground that night, staring at the stars until his mother came and took him home.

He wanted to ask his mother the same question, but the response from his friends discouraged him. He thought that maybe his mother would also give the same reaction, so he decided that it was wise not to ask anything like this to her. From that point on, he thought it was best to stay within himself and be private in his musings.

The next day, one of his friend's mothers came to his house. When Gaurav's mother asked her what the issue was, she said that her son was asking inappropriate questions to his son and the other boys. They are scared of him. His mother got worried and asked Gaurav what had happened. Gaurav told her that when he saw the sky turning from blue to yellow and then to black, he just wondered about the process behind it and how it was done. His mother apologised to the lady and assured her that it would never happen again.

After the lady was gone, Gaurav's mother called him and asked him how come he could think of something so mature. And asked him to not give any attention to such thoughts, as they would make all the other kids afraid of him, and he is too young to be thinking of something this cosmic and universal. She told him that it is all done by God and that you do not question God's doings.

Gaurav agreed and promised that he would never ask such a question to anyone again. But deep inside, Gaurav continued thinking about the question himself. He wanted to know what other people thought of the process.

His mother's words gave birth to a new question in his mind. If it is God's doing, then he must have the answer to his question, and so when he used to find himself alone, he used to ask this question to God. Needless to say, he never got an answer back. So, with time passing, the question began to blur out, and he was soon back to being the child who used to play in the town with other kids.

Gaurav would go on to understand later that parents and caregivers must be aware of their child's present stage of intellect. If they are able to appreciate the depth of thought and uniqueness of the child's vision, they could provide activities that will aid in the child's cognitive or intellectual development.

To most parents, intellectual or cognitive growth in their child is all related to the level of developing academic skills and expanding their knowledge base. Recognising the colour, learning the alphabet, and, of course, knowing how to read, write, and learning arithmetic are usually the extent they consider when it comes to intelligence and intellectuality.

Cognitive and intellectual growth, on the other hand, is significantly broader. Cognitive and intellectual development are both concerned with how changes in the brain affect how we think and learn as we grow. Children do not simply know less than adults. There are distinctions in how they think about and comprehend their experiences as well.

Like Gaurav was, many children are inherently curious and begin to explore and experiment as they grow older, building their knowledge base and skill set. It will not be very wrong to think of them as "little scientists" in some ways. Had Gaurav the maturity that only comes with age, he would have thought himself to be so.

Young children are not much different from explorers. They possess curiosity, learn new things and collect the knowledge they obtain from trying new things through playing and making contact with others in their environment. This was one of the reasons that despite being quiet and thoughtful, Gaurav was interested in his friends and the games they played. He was vaguely conscious since there is a difference between the things people are taught and the things which they learn on their own. For instance, learning to speak a language simply by being in the surroundings of people who communicate in that language is different to learning to pass the academic exams by memorising.

As a youngster tries to make sense of their ever-expanding surroundings, there are two processes that they go through.

One is assimilation, which is the process through which children make sense of their surroundings. They use the knowledge they already possess and resort to extending its reach. It entails integrating their current cognitive structure with reality and their experiences. As a result, a child's grasp of how the universe works filters and shapes their interpretation of reality.

It will be wrong to say that children simply absorb knowledge passively. They are no sponges; Gaurav could see that much by observing even his lesser thoughtful friends. He and the other children around him were continually creating new thoughts and experimenting with those concepts in order to make sense of the universe.

This Assimilation concept can well be understood in how children recognise different types of animals. Take an example of a donkey. To a child, anything which is a large, four-legged animal would be a donkey if all they have been told about is a donkey. A cow and horse, by this logic, both become a donkey. As the kid encounters new knowledge in the world, it is then he can begin to integrate into the existing representation of various four-legged animals.

The second example is of equilibration. Children establish a balance between assimilation and accommodation as they begin to grow and observe. Equilibration helps youngsters like Gaurav to strike a balance between using their prior knowledge and modifying their behaviour in response to new information. That is the way of the world, one takes in the newly found information and combines it with the knowledge one already has. Making little tweaks to the existing knowledge can help differentiate the two things.

Gaurav had the habit of observing and thinking of the things which were not in clear sight, things that were more metaphysical in nature. Such as, he used to think of life and wonder why everyone works. Why do they all struggle and build a life for themselves when they are going to die one day. He wanted to ask his parents and elders these questions, but they seemed to be enjoying their lives way too much. So, he concluded that maybe it is only because he is just a child. Once he grew older, he will also understand the real meaning of life and will learn to love it for whatever purpose.

But the question remained there. He tried to shake it off his head, but his mind kept on going to it again and again whenever he found himself alone with his thoughts. But slowly, with time, he got busy with school, friends, studies, and eventually, this question also began to blur away.

His family started facing financial issues because of his father's job and rising expenses. He used to earn minimum, and the wage was not a regular wage either. Also, due to his father constantly switching jobs, it was not easy to save and invest.

Gaurav used to observe his parents argue about money all the time. His father used to ask his mother to limit her spending, and she used to ask him to look for a better and secure job. But deep down, he had no idea why money was such a big issue. He used to think that why can't the government just print money and give it to the poor people.

Pretty soon, he realised that his parents were arguing about money because they wanted to send Gaurav to a big school where he could get a better education. Gaurav found this reason to be very lame. He would walk around in parks with hands in his pockets, kicking stones just thinking about this. At that age, he was not bothered about which school he goes. However, he was surprised and confused that everybody around him knew which school he should go to and what he should study. He was not sure what to do.

"How come these people know what is best for me, and which school should I be going to?" He was least bothered about it, and turned his face towards the sky.

Chapter 2: The Door to a Big School

Gaurav was still not able to function the stress his family was putting on him. They were making him study day and night just so he could pass the test to the big school. He did everything they asked him to do. He studied like a fifteen-year-old. Each subject is being installed in his brain by his family. Even though it looked like Gaurav was working very hard and studying all day but in the back of his head he was still deep into his thoughts. Thinking about why his family is pushing him so hard. Why do they want him to go to the big school? And again, how do they know what is good for him? The one person who was calm throughout this process was his grandfather *(dadu)*. He used to say to him, "Don't worry about whatever happens because you will go to a school anyway."

But in general society, children so young are not expected to ask questions and allowed to make decisions on their own. The adults believe that because they are children, they cannot make wise decisions and that they will end up creating a huge problem for themselves. So, it is believed that their parents should be making the decisions related to their lives. But Gaurav thought otherwise. He thought that his life decisions should be his responsibility and that others could only think about what was good for him. They cannot give the surety as for him he just wanted to continue at the same school where he had made some good friends and thought that it would abruptly end.

Finally, the entrance exam day was here. In the morning, before he was leaving for the exam, his mother did the aarti and gave him a sweet. It is a ritual in Hinduism, where they soak wicks in ghee and then offer them to Gods by lighting them up, wishing that the Gods will grant their wish. She then applied a red tika on Gaurav's forehead and then let him go.

Gaurav's father took him to the school on his scooter. He was sent in with other kids to a classroom. There they were all given a series of things to do, such as writing an essay. Recognising shapes, basic maths, names of countries and capitals, recognising animals, etc. To Gaurav, he thought that he was not that good. He looked at other children who were doing way better than him. But he did not care much and kept on doing the tasks in a way which he found suitable. After the test was done, he came out, and his father was still waiting. He walked to his father and when he asked him about how the test went. Gaurav replied by saying that it went fine. But deep inside, he was doubtful whether he would be able to pass it or not. He did not let this thought worry him much, and he came back home.

A few weeks went by, and the results were still not out. Gaurav's family was getting worried about whether he passed the test or not. On the other hand, Gaurav was occupied with playing and roaming around the town. His father used to go the school every day asking if the results were out or not. But the school kept on telling him that the results would be announced by next week.

One day, his mother prepared the food and was waiting for Gaurav's father to come. They waited all evening, but there was no sign of him. Phones were not an easy accessory to afford in those times. So, all she could do was wait. Her husband finally came home after a few hours, and to her surprise, he brought the news which they both had been waiting for. Their son had passed the test, and he will be going to the big school. So, Gaurav's father brought sweets for his family to celebrate the good news.

They told Gaurav about it, and instead of being happy like them, Gaurav was surprised. He did not expect that it as he thought the exam did not go that well. But then he thought that maybe this is all God's doing. God wants him to go to the big school and help his family, maybe. So, he did not worry about it much and embraced the good news with open arms.

Even though he had accepted that it was all God's doing, he still could not shake away the thought of how he got qualified. Also, one thing that confused him was why every other person was getting happy, why people were coming to his house congratulating him, and being so happy that Gaurav got into the big school. Because it was him who got into the big school, it will be him studying there. Why were the relatives so happy then? His parents were telling everyone that they were blessed with a genius child and that their bad days would be over soon. Now that their son will go to a big school.

This not knowing was annoying for him as he used to think that he was missing something. He could not understand why elders were so happy about something that he had to do. But anyway, life went on. He knew he had to go to school and study, but he was happier because he was with friends, and it was fun. He still had this deep quietness which made people think that he was a very quiet person, but the quietness was not planned. It came because he had this feeling of not knowing what was going on. He would realise in the future that this quietness was his biggest strength and not his weakness which everybody else around him used to tell him.

So, he started going to the big school with his friends. He was a bright student in the first few years. He was being ranked among the top three students of his class, and his academic score was also good. Gaurav's parents were proud of their son. They were happy. They appreciated his hard work and motivated him to perform better in the next year.

In school, there are all sorts of students. Each one with his own abilities and qualities. They are unique in their own way, but still, there are some qualities that let people, especially teachers, classify them into different groups. See to which type they belong to. Some of these types are:

1. Hard-Workers

They are always motivated. They are aware of their goals, and they also know the ways to acquire them. However, you do not count them as the smart kind, but they are capable of pulling out wonders if they are motivated and pushed in the right direction.

2. Clowns

These are the kids who always try to make the whole class laugh with their jokes. Sometimes they are funny. Sometimes they are not. They want to keep the environment of the class very lively. They sometimes get punished for this, too, but it gives them satisfaction.

3. Nerds

These students can be spotted in a lonely corner, sitting with their books, all the time. They believe that books are their best friends. They do not ask any questions. They do not bully. Books give you extreme knowledge and make you intelligent.

4. Bullies

The bullies are the gangsters of the school. They are the highest on the hierarchy of the students because they are strong and they know how to push others down. Other students do not try to confront them either because they are afraid that they might get into trouble for doing so.

While at school, Gaurav started making more friends. At his school, there were two categories of students. One with a good academic score, who were invested in studies all the time. And the other, who were sorted as naughty boys or the backbenchers in the class. They were busy in all sorts of activities, other than studying. Everybody expected Gaurav to be friends with the academic students, as he was so quiet all the time. But to their surprise, he soon became friends with everyone at school. Be it the students with good academic scores or the other group of students.

But as he grew older, things started getting more difficult for him as he could not be around both group at one time. He had to choose whether to be with the studious group or with the fun games group. This started worrying him because leaving one group of friends for another was something completely new to him. And this feeling of abandoning one side was killing him from the inside. He particularly did not like the fact that he had to choose between his friends, although he saw no difference between them. He started getting more interested in extracurricular activities compared to studying. And he was more inclined to the group of naughty students than the one with a good academic score.

This started affecting his academics. At first, he was being ranked in the top three students by the end of the year. But with his company being changed from studious to pranksters. He began to gloom out. His academic score started going down. But it was still good. He was not failing in any of his classes, but this still made his parents angry at him. They told him to work hard and get back into the top three because, to them, it was disappointing. They also started to get worried that what if Gaurav failed. Then all their hard work will go into the vein, and their expectations of Gaurav becoming financially stable will turn into dust. But when they used to look at the results of other kids in the family, they used to feel better and hopeful that Gaurav was still performing better than them, and he will gain the ranking back.

Whereas for Gaurav, he was happy with what he was doing at that moment. He was involved in pranks and naughty activities. His academic score was above average, and it was satisfactory for him. He was not much concerned about it, though. The feeling of emptiness inside him had somehow stopped bugging him. All those questions in his head stopped disturbing him because his investment in other activities took over. He was enjoying himself. To him, being surrounded by studious kids was sort of boring because all they did was study and worry about their academics. In comparison, the naughty kids were involved in all fun activities, whether it be games, parties, or pulling out pranks on others.

All this gave birth to new thoughts in Gaurav's head when he saw his parents getting angry at him for not securing a good position in the class, but praising him in front of others and telling him that they are proud of him when they compared his grades with other kids in the family. All this made Gaurav confused. He began to think that what the matter with him was. Is he okay or not? Is he doing well, or is he doing badly in class? But he did not let the thought worry him that much. So, he went on with his studies and other activities altogether, without taking too much pressure on.

As he was getting promoted to the next class every year, he could not fully understand what the promotion was for? Was this for just passing the exam as he never really finished reading all the books from the previous class. Each year he was being introduced to new subjects such as economics, math, and science as well. And his understanding of the world started to develop as well. By the age of thirteen or fourteen, he started to notice a change within himself. He felt that his beliefs were changing a little bit. But he could not understand what the change was exactly. And he could not speak to anyone about this because he himself was not able to understand the root cause of the sudden change within him. Because they were just random thoughts. So, he would just ignore them and go on with day-to-day daily activities.

But the change and the new thoughts remained there. Gaurav came from a very religious family, but was always confused and doubtful about God. They used to celebrate all the festivals in the Hindu calendar and pray every day for good luck and betterment. His whole family used to go temple regularly, and his mom used to perform pooja twice every day. So, telling them that he has doubts about God and that he kind of questions his existence would have been a great shock to his parents. This might also lead to some major consequences. So, Gaurav stayed quiet and did not talk to anyone about this.

He used to go to the temple with his family, but he had no idea what he should pray for because he was confused about whether God will even listen to him or not. His parents had told him the stories of all the great Gods in Hinduism, but they were all stories to him, like any other. But questioning this would have been a risk. So, Gaurav kept on doing what he was asked to do. He used to go to the temple.

He used to perform pooja. He used to fast and do other things. But deep inside, he knew that he did not believe in any of it.

There were a few big temples in his town which are usual in most places in India. Gaurav used to love the temple environment because usually, it used to be a gathering of families and with a lot of spaces with trees and gardens to play around. He was never much interested in the puja itself. He would notice that outside the temples, there would be hundreds of beggars, usually on the big occasions and similarly hundreds of rich people who come to the temple in the cars. The people who visit the temples would give some change to the beggar outside but leave hundreds of rupees next to an idol inside. Gaurav, of course, understood people believed in God, so they did what they did, he was never fully convinced and would always think, what if all the money given to the temple was equally distributed amongst the beggars and it solved a lot of their problems. So he thought, *Why can't money be just printed and given to all it's man-made after all?*

The question about the money was still in his head. He still used to think about it over and over that how something which is made by men cannot be just circulated around to people who need it. Because everything in the world revolves around money, people respect you if you have money and will not even talk to you if you are poor. Why is money so important in the world? All these questions made him interested in economics during his school days because he wanted to find out everything about money. The origin, how it is printed, where is it printed, and why it cannot be printed enough to be circulated? But basic economics failed to answer any of his questions.

At the same time, throughout his school life, the financial issues remained. His father was earning minimal wages, but it was not enough to pay for the school on time. At Gaurav's school, they had the policy that the student could continue his studies throughout the year without paying the fee. But when the year ends they have to pay the full fee, in order to receive the result and move to the next class. So, it used to be a challenge every year, but by the end of the year, his father was able to manage from somewhere and pay the fee. This kept on happening for all the years that Gaurav studied there. His father used to borrow money or used to find some funds, so he could pay the fee. This whole thing used to worry Gaurav as he wanted to continue his school.

Gaurav's family was concerned about his studies. They told him to focus on his studies and get good grades. They wanted him to study hard and earn good marks so he can be counted as one of the best students in the school. But to Gaurav, the major concern was about something else. His concern was about the money. Because throughout his childhood to his teen, he has seen his family struggling for money. He did not want that to happen, and this worried him, as a huge amount of earnings was being spent on his fee every year.

At the age of fourteen, Gaurav started thinking about money in a very serious manner. He understood that they needed money, and it is the only way to solve their problems. Every night he used to lay down in his bed and think of how he could make money. He used to have this feeling that in the future, he would make a lot of money. He will become a rich man, he will earn well and all their financial problems will be history after that because everything in your life was because of money.

Gaurav's family were peaceful people. They never got into any disputes. They were strong supporters of peace, and they believed that fighting was just another reason to spread negativity. They used to go to temples and pray the majority of the time. And his parents used to love him. So, there was no factor of hatred in Gaurav's life. But there was one thing that he was made to fear throughout his childhood. Whenever he was around any elder from his family, in a gathering, and especially when alone, he would get a lot of advice on life and what he needed to do. The narrative was the same for everyone, study hard and well, or his future would not be a happy one. He will live a life of a poor person. He will either get the job of a bus conductor, or he will have a small store in the town, just like other people. The concept was that study hard and find a job as if there was no other way to earn a living. In a subtle way, this was the fear of failure that was being instilled into him from a very young age.

Gaurav, however, did not think about what others were saying. He did not get angry or shout or argue with people. It was just not him. He used to listen to all of their advice but never gave them any thought. He was never concerned about what others were doing or what they had to say.

Although all these pieces of advice were contradictory, they set up Gaurav's basic mindset. Regarding everything, he needed to be successful in his life. A good job, money, and a secured future. This made him understand that there is nothing more important than money in life. He realised that you have to earn if you want to survive in the world. And build a successful, wealthy life for yourself. Because if you are not wealthy, you cannot be happy.

Chapter 3: Struggle through the Teens

Early teens was a very enjoyable experience for Gaurav. This was the time when he started making sense of the world around him. Well, that is not to say he didn't before, but now he perceived life around him quite deeply. He would observe the people, their behaviours, their attitudes, and the events taking place around him and form his opinions. He was in a phase of life where he was learning, unlearning, and relearning things fast.

Early teens is an age where a child undergoes multiple changes in their thought process. Gaurav was no different from the others in that regard. He was at a stage where his external environment was having an impact on his beliefs and perceptions.

Just like any child in India, Gaurav was a diehard fan of Bollywood movies. Dancing to the tune of high beat songs was a recurring thing in the lives of Indians. Not just songs, music, as a whole, is a recurrent theme in the everyday lives of most people there. None of the functions, be it weddings, routine celebrations, or religious festivals, were complete without thunderous rounds of drum beating followed by crazy moves of a group of people dancing around.

This was also the time when cable and cinemas were gaining popularity with the public. There would be advertisements all around the roads featuring some Indian actors in sharp colours and vivid backgrounds. While the popular culture was casting deep imprints on the minds of the people, there were some like Gaurav who were looking at these developments from a different angle.

One day, Gaurav realised that popular TV shows, dramas, and movies had an impact on everybody around. People started thinking and feeling the way they saw the characters on the TV doing. That was followed by another realisation that most people only followed what they observed or what was played before their eyes, to be more precise. Most of the things we saw were mere performances.

Gaurav thought to himself that everybody wanted to be a hero, but nobody wanted to give it what it took. Most people were exceptional at dancing, for instance, but to speak the truth, if those people were adept at something, it was copying. They copied their favourite actors instead of inventing something of their own.

Gaurav thought this was a weird realisation. The reason for that was that he himself was going through the same process and was no different from the large majority. Gaurav wasn't good at singing and dancing and just tried to copy what he saw on the TV. He thought if he did that nicely, he'd become a sort of an expert in dancing. Some of his friends were very good at copying those dance moves they saw on popular media. He enjoyed watching them, but he knew they were just trying to copy someone else and not producing anything original.

This was really a subtle thought. As time went by, Gaurav realised that everything they did as a society was in one way or another copied and based on cinema and characters that were shown in the movies. Young Gaurav could see that the media was, in a way, telling people what they should do and how they should do it.

Back at school, Gaurav was exploring his interest and strengths. In his early teens, he was very good at studies, especially math used to be his favourite subject. He was a huge fan of painting as well. He was not a big fan of science, though. He enjoyed economics more than physics, chemistry, and other natural sciences. The school was a mixed experience. Gaurav loved some courses, while he did not find the others as interesting.

Throughout his early teens, financial issues haunted Gaurav's family. As they grew up, their expenses multiplied many times. His parents barely managed household expenses plus those of his education, which included school fees, tuition fees, stationery, and other supplies. Gaurav's brother was also growing up during this time. As he progressed at school, his expenses added up.

Gaurav had been very close to him right from childhood and through teens. Part of the reason for that was the boys had a very strict environment at home. They were brought up in a rather rigid system. As children, they were never allowed to hang out with friends outside or loiter around the neighbourhood. They were only expected to go as far as school. After school timings, they were expected to stay at home and dedicate whatever time they had to their studies.

Gaurav had few options when it came to recreation. He spent most of the time with his brother, who was also his playing buddy. The two of them would watch cartoons together. They would huddle around the TV to watch whatever show was airing. They would play board games for long hours. They would also read comics together and burst into fits of laughter when something hilarious caught their eyes.

The brotherly bond grew stronger with time. Facing a difficult financial situation, the two young boys became best friends. On the other hand, their father was looking for stability in his life. When he was a little better, he started looking for employment opportunities in some short-term projects outside of the town. He wanted a break from the people he was working with then as there wasn't much-earning potential to support their growing needs there.

The job hunt came to a halt when Gaurav's father landed a good job in a nearby industrial city. This place was about five hours of distance if travelled through the train. Going that far and living without family was not so easy, but Gaurav's parents decided to go for it. After all, they had been desperately looking for a job, and not many times they manage to get a good one.

This new place was good. Gaurav's father was happy; he had a stable job. He stayed in the city of his posting for the most part and would come home every two or three weeks for the weekend. This continued for a few months. As hard as it was living away from their father, there was some silver lining that kept them happy. For instance, there was a regular supply of money coming in every month, and that brought solace and comfort to them.

Gaurav, along with his family, used to miss his father a lot. For as long as he could remember, his father had not really stayed away from the house since Gaurav's birth. Naturally, they felt a sense of emptiness with him missing. Everything he owned or had in use reminded them of him, and the emotions of love surged an all-time high at the sight of his belonging.

The distance between Gaurav's family and his father was enhanced by a lack of connectivity between the two. There was not much access to the internet in the town at that time, but Gaurav's family did not even have a phone. So, his father used to call on their neighbour's phone and request them to call their family next door. Excited to talk to him, Gaurav and his family would come running to the neighbour's telephone, taking turns to have a conversation with his father.

In those short conversations, Gaurav's father would check on the family and ascertain everything was alright. He would send his love and prayers via call, and his family would return to their home with smiles on their faces. That became a ritual. One of the best times in weeks was when their father called.

He had loads of relatives around him in the form of uncles, aunties, cousins, etc. In fact, a large part of their relatives was settled in the same city. Whenever they felt lonely, they realised they could contact their relatives. That thought brought much solace to them in this difficult time. They knew if they were in any trouble, there were people to offer them a helping hand. So, they were never alone. There were few people in the city they could count on.

At this time, what bothered Gaurav the most was his mother's sadness. From a very young age, he had seen his mother sacrificing everything for the sake of running the family perfectly. She was the woman who would always put her husband and children before her without uttering a word in complaint. The same woman was now unhappy and worried about their financial situation. Their meagre finances and troubling times had made her upset. Gaurav, being close to his mother, could not help getting affected by that.

Gaurav could see his mother was not enjoying her life at all. If anything, he wanted to console his mother and give her the best of everything and alleviate all her worries. However, there was nothing in his hands. Things remained the same in the next few months until the day came when his father completed the duration defined in the contract. This was the beginning of another difficult phase.

Gaurav's family started facing financial challenges all over again. His father tried his luck with getting the contract renewed but to no avail. Ultimately, he had to let go of this temporary job. The only option he was left with now was to look for another job, which he did eventually. He stayed in the same town and began hunting for a job again.

Meanwhile, Gaurav was super excited to be on his own. This was the first time he was living without their father. He had nobody to dictate his terms on him. He could do everything he wanted. He was free and had no fear of being rebuked. He could go out, come late at night because there was nobody to keep a handle on him. Gaurav was enjoying one of his first flavours of liberty, and he did not want it to end.

Life is never all good. There were some painful experiences too haunting Gaurav's family in those months.

The bitterest memory he has from that time is seeing his mother receiving some threatening comments from the debtors. They did not have a house of their own and were living in rented accommodation. So, now when they were unable to pay the rent for a couple of months, the house owner would come at their door, demanding the deferred rent. Among the debtors were also grocery shop owners who had given some grocery items to the family as loans.

Surely, when these people were not paid back in a long time, they would get rather coarse and would resort to insulting Gaurav's mother. Young Gaurav would hear the conversations between them, and he felt as if someone had stabbed him right in his chest. The mental trauma he went through once kept playing in his mind again and again and would keep him stressed for days. Gaurav often reflected on the words of the debtors on his bed and felt bad for being in this position.

One of the most terrible encounters Gaurav had was with the person who was a childhood friend of his father. This man owed him some money and would pay a visit at least two or three times a week. Gaurav did not know much about it since his dad never discussed such matters with the kids. Hence, he would not pay them much attention either. However, this one time he came, he shook Gaurav and his family to the core.

What happened was this man came and asked to see Gaurav's father. Upon finding out that he had not been around, he asked Gaurav to bring a pen and paper. Gaurav complied and showed up with a writing pad and a pen just moments later. Next, the man asked him, "Could you please write something down for your dad on my behalf since my arm is aching today." Gaurav quickly responded with a naïve "Sure!" He went on, "Write. You owe me Rs. 10,000 (£ 100 approx.). I need the amount ASAP. And tell me one thing, why do you lie so much? Do you even lie this much at your home?"

The comment sent pangs of embarrassment down Gaurav's spine. He did not quite get the intention of that man back then; he just knew he hurled a terrible insult at his father. Now that he looks back at it, he realises he was trying to humiliate his father in front of him. Ironically, Gaurav's father used to call this man 'his oldest friend'. On that day, one thing came through very clearly that this man was worse than an enemy. He was only interested in money; nothing or nobody mattered to him more than that. This was a very big realisation as he instantly knew that the same could happen with him and his friends as well.

As humiliating as the comment was, Gaurav tried to stay calm and composed in the face of it. He threw the paper away immediately after that man left and only informed his father that this man came and reminded him how he owed him Rs. 10,000. That was the end of it. Gaurav does not remember what became of it. All he remembers is that this one incident left a deep impact on his thoughts.

Gaurav could not help thinking about it and feeling bad. His feelings changed from humiliation to worry to anger, at times. It was not so much the words or the individual that incited anger and hatred in him. It was the circumstances that his family was facing that caused resentment. Gaurav would deliberate upon it for days to come. He kept thinking about his circumstances and comparing them with those of his friends and, ultimately, came to the conclusion that making money was extremely important. Only when you had ample money in your hands could you live a respectable life.

Gaurav desperately wanted to ease the situation for his family, but there was hardly anything he could do. He knew that at the age of fifteen, he had no chances of earning money, no matter how badly he wanted to. He wanted to help his parents with the finances. At best, he could only focus on his studies more. That was the only thing he could do at the age to please his parents. However, deep down inside, Gaurav had internalised the idea that the only goal in life was to earn lots of money.

When he became seventeen, Gaurav had changed quite a lot in terms of his ambitions. He had a vast friends circle. A lot of them were mostly average students who were not really interested in studies. Most of them belonged to wealthy families and had big businesses to look after once they grew up. Their lifestyle was lavish, the exact opposite of Gaurav's. They would often remark, "What's the point of studying at all? I mean, I just need a degree so that I can show it to people and throw it in the bin when it has fulfilled its purpose. After all, I'm going to manage my father's business in the future."

For Gaurav, on the other hand, getting a good education was a matter of survival in this world. That was the only way he could raise his social status and live a respectable life. That was what he was told back at home always. However, his friends believed they only needed to get a good degree so that they could marry in an affluent family and receive a good dowry. The bigger the degree, the more the dowry. In India, marriage was no very similar to a business deal. The matter was decided upon by careful analysis of profits and losses.

In a desperate attempt at improving his future, Gaurav turned to his studies because he knew he did not have any inheritance to count on. In fact, he had the responsibility of supporting his family when he grew up. Gaurav wanted to study well, get a scholarship and go to a big college so that he could make something out of himself.

The financial situation he was in could not afford him the money to go to a good college. The only way he could afford higher education was by getting a scholarship. But for that, he would have to study hard and get exceptional grades. At the same time, however, he wasn't sure what he wanted to do in his life. He had a hard time picking a career. Every time he sat to study, random questions regarding his future bothered his mind, and he could not pay much attention to the textbook.

Perhaps due to this confusion, he could not fare well in his academic results. At the age of sixteen, he got poor grades in his final exams that concerned his parents. The results of the ninth and tenth standards were crucial in deciding the career path of the child. Parents in India would spend so much of their savings to afford the best coaching academies for their children. They had high hopes of them. That was because these grades were instrumental in getting admission to colleges.

Seeing Gaurav performing poorly in the exam, his parents were extremely unhappy. They had expected him to perform better, and Gaurav felt their pain. He never wanted to make them sad. However, the result was not something out of the blue. On a personal level, Gaurav was expecting similar grades because he had worked barely hard enough.

In his entire sixteenth year, the most fun time Gaurav had was with his friends and social networks. He would love to meet them and spend time with them as they had all the facilities required to go out and have fun. All friends had bikes or cars, and at the time, there was nothing more exciting than driving and roaming around for usually no reason, but just because all of them were new drivers.

Usually, Gaurav would run out of money, but a couple of friends would cover him if needed. Sometimes he would stay back home as he would run out of money and wait till he got it again. He fancied the lifestyle and assets his rich friends had mainly because he knew that it was possible to do something material in life, and he resolved to find a way to make a good future for himself. One of his friends used to have a huge bungalow, and whenever he was in his house, he often asked himself, "Would I ever live in a house like this one?" He knew that his parents and family thought that his friends' circle was a huge problem as it impacted his academic career. However, he saw his friends' lifestyle (especially the rich families) as something that gave him direction, motivation, and hope to achieve something bigger that what his family didn't even think about.

Chapter 4: Good Days Are Here! But not for Long

There is a saying that, "Things do not stay the same always." At some point, it seems like a set of words that does not make any sense, but to some, it is hope. A hope that they are going to make it out of their misery and that they will one day have what their heart desires. And that hope is what keeps them going on and on until they come face-to-face with their desire. They then look it in the eye and smile. But change does not happen overnight. It takes time, and it happens gradually.

To Gaurav, that change had finally started happening. He still remembered the time when his father's so-called best friend came to their house and said those cruel things about his father. At that time, he could not do anything, even though he wanted to, but he did not. It was still with him, those words, that tone, and his expressions. But he never let it affect him. He did not tell his father about the event because he did not want him to worry more.

For a month, they had no contact from Gaurav's father. His mother used to worry and pray all the time for his well-being. Praying to Gods that keep him safe and bring him back to them even with no success. Gaurav and his brother also used to think of their father and worry whether he was safe or not because that was all they could do. They did not have a phone, so there was no room to contact him, and they could not just go out on a blind search. So, they decided to wait for a few more weeks. If they still do not hear anything from their father, then they will go to the police and file a missing person report.

Those days passed very slowly. Now, it was worrying Gaurav as well. He wanted to go out and look for his father. His uncles were there to support and try to make some contact with the company he worked for. Also, back then, telephones did not use to show the number on them, and you had to contact the operator if you wanted to get the number. So, he had no idea of what to do. All this worry was affecting his studies as well. His friends used to comfort him and give hope to him that his father must be fine, and he would contact them.

And finally, one day, he did. Gaurav and his family were having dinner when suddenly there was a drastic knock on their door. He immediately ran and checked. It was their neighbour. "Yes? What happened?" Gaurav asked, and he asked them to come quickly because their father had called. They all left the food immediately and went running to his house. His mother took the phone, and as soon as she heard her husband's voice, she broke into tears. They talked, and he told her about everything. He told her that he had found a new job and it is paying very well that is the reason he was totally occupied for the last few weeks. Because he used to come back late every night and leave so early that he did not have the time to call. He also said that he had saved a lot of money and he was going to send it to them. Then he talked to Gaurav and told him that he would send the money and asked Gaurav to return it to all the people he had lent money from.

But unfortunate for Gaurav and his family, a few weeks after the call, Gaurav's father came back. When asked what happened to his job and he said that the company hired him only for a few months and that as soon as his contract ended, he was let go. We would only know after few months that his contract ended because he seriously injured himself at work, but never informed us as we would get worried. He did not know what else to do, so he came back. Gaurav was shocked as he knew that this will bring all the same problems back.

All this brought back the deep thinking and all the questions he used to have about the world. Gaurav realised that his family was back on the same track they were a few months ago, on the hunt for money again. Gaurav's father told him not to worry about it. He assured him that he had some savings and he would find a job before those savings came to an end. Gaurav believed him, but he could not help himself. The question regarding the *importance of money was back. He again started to wonder why something made by humans could not be just given to people for free,* why people cannot print as much money as they want.

Gaurav finally had a realisation that his father was trying more than he could, but it was not enough because their expenses were increasing. He realised that his father needed an extra hand. He needs someone who can also bring money to the house. So, he decided to step up and become a helping hand to his father. Gaurav was a good student at school. He wanted to go to a good college, but he knew that his family would not have enough money to send him to a private college. So, he decided to give out tuition to other students. That way, he believed that he would be able to take care of his expenses, and his father would be able to save for his college. And to his surprise, it went pretty well. He started with a group of three students, and soon the numbers began to increase, and he was overwhelmed. Because being a teenager and teaching others closer to his age was not something he ever imagined. Also, the feeling of being addressed as 'sir' was very overwhelming to him.

Gaurav's friends mostly had a rich family background compared to him. They were all pretty well-off, and they did not have much to worry about the future. Where Gaurav was constantly told to focus on his studies to have any chance in the future, his friends were partying and relaxing at their cosy homes. They used to tell him that there was no point in studying too hard as in the future they are simply going to join their father's business and make a living by taking care of it for the rest of their life. They only needed the degree so they could get married.

At that time in India, the conception of dowry was very common, and people used to support the idea. What happens in dowry is that the bride's side of the family presents a lot of things demanded by the groom's side. It could be money, item, car, and even a house. He saw this prevalent in many families around him.

The more educated you are, the chances are that you will receive a big dowry.

But for Gaurav, the situation was different. His family was not that rich, and he did not have his father's business to rely on. He had to make his own future, work for it and build it because there was no other way around it. The only option he had was to study hard, score well and get a scholarship if he wished to get into a good college. All this pressure affected his academics. He got so confused with all the hopes and dreams to fulfil that when the result came, his marks were near average. It was pretty catastrophic for his parents, and they did not expect this from him. But Gaurav, on the other hand, was completely aware of what he deserved, and he believed that this was it. So, Gaurav did not get the scholarship, and he had to go to a public college and continue his tuition for almost two years. Tuition was a good getaway for Gaurav, he was loved, and he was being respected. All his students used to love his teaching style. Gaurav used to play games with them, never get angry at them, and kept on motivating them to work harder. All that effort paid off when the results came out, and all of his students had gotten excellent marks. Gaurav was proud of himself and of his students. He knew that he was capable of inspiring others and that his guidance would help his students to be successful.

He was earning one thousand rupees from the tuition, which was a lot. He got to save, give his share to the household and also lend his friends some if they needed. One thing he did not enjoy because of the tuition was to miss his evening activities. Before tuition, Gaurav used to go with his friends to the playground to play games. They used to hang out, go to places, and chill, but since the tuition, he had not been able to do that. He loved playing badminton, but due to this, he had to miss it too.

As now he had some money, Gaurav and his cousin Jitu went to Kolkata on holiday. This was the first time ever he travelled on a train, and he was head over heels. He went to the city for the first time and found a number of new things. But to Gaurav, the train journey was something he was never going to forget. The reason was his love for trains since he was five. This was the time of happiness and of pride to Gaurav because he did not ask his father for any money. He arranged everything from his own earnings, and this made him feel good.

Gaurav was seventeen years old, and some of his friends already had girlfriends. This was a prominent age to have girlfriends and have relationships. Because this is what every teen at this age do, they date, they fall in love, get heartbroken. It was a very exciting time for the whole group because the boys with girlfriends used to tell the others about what it is like being in a relationship and having a girlfriend. Gaurav used to wish that he had a girlfriend too. So, he could talk about her to his friends and tell them how good she is and other things. But he never did anything about it because when the thought of having a girlfriend used to cross his mind, he also began to think that having a girlfriend was another added expense. You are supposed to take your girlfriend out, take her to dinner, and get gifts for her. So, these things made him wonder if can he even have a girlfriend, and he never gave it a shot without actually knowing for himself what it was going to be like.

So, instead of going out and exploring his dating life, Gaurav used to help his friends. He used to help them with the selection of restaurants. He used to drop them off and pick them up after their dates. This was fun sometimes. His company with his richer friends inspired him a lot. They taught him what the essential things in life are. He saw how it felt like having three to four cars outside your house, having multiple servants, eating outside, getting fancy clothes, going to clubs with friends, and other things.

Gaurav always found these activities much more exciting than the usual things his family used to do, which always pushed him to focus on studies and to get a job and get settled. There was no room for any fun activities. And even if they had any sort of fun, it was bound by a number of rules, which totally killed the buzz.

Gaurav used to visit his friend's house very often. Their families used to like him as well. He was a good kid. He knew how to talk to his elders and how to behave. They used to treat him as their own son. By being around them he could already see the advantages of having money. He could see the luxury of life his friends had because they were very well-off. This soon started coming to him that the money he was making from the tuition was not enough. Not like his friends asked him to spend as much as them, but he could feel it himself. Most of his company at that time were boys, who were taking care of their father's business and were having fun, going out with their girlfriends, partying, and doing all sorts of things that were never done in Gaurav's house.

This looked like an absolute panicle to him at that time, so in his mind, he already had decided that he must have a business to earn more money. But for that, he needed some investment because the tuition fees he got was not enough to make an investment. As he was already thinking about so many things, he lost his focus from his own studies. Gaurav passed his school with average marks, and the same happened with the college. He used to go there, but he did not focus that much. Ultimately, by the end of the year, he used to manage to secure average marks, enough to get him to the next class, and that was enough for him.

He found it very funny that his parents wanted him to be a studious guy who secured great marks, got a great scholarship, and passed the bank entrance exam. But Gaurav turned out to be completely the opposite of what they were expecting him to be academic wise. Although he always remained quiet and well behaved. Given the type of friends he had, he was now starting to go to bars to have an occasional drink and smoke. This is where he and his friends will make plans to start their own business, which was completely opposite of what his parents wanted him to do. When he proposed the idea to his parents, they had mixed feelings because they saw that their son was at least trying to do something. So, they supported him, not wholeheartedly, but they did.

So, with his parent's support and the ambition of making some money to start a business, Gaurav started working at a factory, which one of his father's friends owned. He was an employee there and was getting a small allowance. His father's friend used to tell him all the time that he should not feel like an employee and that Gaurav is like a son to him. But what he used to do was he never gave Gaurav a proper salary, just the allowance, and he kept on telling him to work hard and that if he did, he would one day be able to run and manage the factory. Gaurav used to listen to him and get inspired that this man believed in me. He used to work for ten to eleven hours a day and get some allowance by the end of the day. It was not enough, but it was more than what he was made solely from the tuition. So, he kept doing it. He continued giving tuitions along with work in the factory.

He was super enthusiastic about this. So, he gave it all he had. He used to work like crazy. In fact, soon, he started enjoying his tasks at the factory more, compared to his college studies and tuition. He did it for almost a year. During that year, he made a lot of contacts with the people involved in business, and he also managed to save some amount for himself. At this stage, his parents were still double-minded about what their son was doing. Because they expected him to become a bank manager or software engineer or something like that, and have a great job, but he was working at a factory, with other employees. So, that kept them a little foggy.

Gaurav, on the other hand, was not interested in that at all. To him, the only thing that mattered was making more and more money and achieving the lifestyle he saw his friends living. His parents also realised that atleast he was not wasting his potential. They understood that he had done work for himself and that he was determined to bring change to his life.

After leaving the factory, Gaurav got in touch with the people and started his own business. He used to buy raw materials, like coal and iron ore, and supply them to the factories near his town. This also gave him a lot of exposure. He used to visit various different towns closer to his town and market his products to the factory owners. He immediately noticed that people who were involved in this business were pretty older, and they considered Gaurav as a kid in the beginning because he was just nineteen. But soon, they realised that the kid had the potential.

One of the key problems for Gaurav was his attitude toward the business. It was just the same as it was to other things. He used to take other people's words for commitment and then tried to come up with deals, which were usually considering everyone's benefit. There was no reason to do it any other way as he wanted to create a good reputation in that business. Soon he realised that the world of business was not what he was thinking. It is not all roses and petals, but there are people who will use you as a pawn to get their needs fulfilled.

He had all the freedom at that time. He was not subjected to any rules. And he was earning pretty good from the business. Within a short passage of time, Gaurav had earned so much that he bought a phone for his home and a second-hand bike for himself. Everything was falling into place, and Gaurav was happy and satisfied. But it did not stay like it for long.

Some of the parties from which Gaurav used to buy the raw material began to do fraud with him. What some of his suppliers did was they took the money from him for the material but did not deliver it. This put him in a bad place. The factory owners were blaming Gaurav for it. They began to pressurise Gaurav. They were all rich and powerful people. Some of them even knew Gaurav's father.

These bad transactions affected his business in a very bad way. He had to pay the factory owners from his own pocket, and soon, without him realising, he was under huge debt. Usually, there was a rotation of raw material and money, so the cycle was going smooth, but with these incidents, all the money was going in vain, with no profit. This was the first time he actually understood, what it is the meaning of the word stress. He could not focus on his studies. His family members were bickering about him, blaming him, calling him an inexperienced kid.

Gaurav used to go out and meet with the people he owed money to in the streets. Because he had seen it once that how people get once you are under their debt, and he did not want his family to see any of it. At this point, everything seemed to finish, but somewhere, in the back of his head, Gaurav had this feeling that this was not his end. He had this feeling that soon, a deal was going to knock at his door and take him out of all his problems. Because of this feeling, he took some really risky deals, hoping that they would be in his favour. But they did not, and again due to his involvement with some dishonest people, whose business was only to make fraud with others, stoke him bad.

It was all hard, but Gaurav was still not ready to blame those people. He thought that maybe it was some of his actions that made those people take these steps. He kept looking for more opportunities. By this time, the news of Gaurav's situation had already reached his father. Some of the factory owners contacted him, asking that if Gaurav is not able to cover the amount, then he has to pay them back.

This all was affecting Gaurav in a bad way. He had lost his vision. He used to go out with his friends, smoking and drinking most of the time as he would feel lost. For the first time, he would truly know what being stressed and worried is, and he would not be able to sleep at night worrying about the consequences of not being able to make up for the losses. This was nothing like worrying about an exam or test, this was dealing with money, and everyone around me in my business circle had left him to deal with the issues. He was hoping for a miracle to happen and take things back to the way they were. What he thought was going to be the gateway to this success felt like the biggest disappointment, especially as he was being ridiculed by most people he knew. But then his father came to his rescue, the only person or option he had left. He paid some of Gaurav's debt and helped Gaurav pay the rest of them. Seeing his son's condition, that he was heartbroken and that he might try his luck in such business again. He decided to send Gaurav to another city for higher studies. He decided to send Gaurav as far away as possible from all this, where he could have a fresh start. So, he arranged some money from here and there and sent his son to Hyderabad.

Chapter 5: New City... New Me

If there is one thing we are sure about in life, it's uncertainty. Life is strange. It's like a road that can lead you forward, backward, make you fly up the sky or drag you down into a deep pit only so you discover a whole new world there. In such a ride, having a plan does help at times, but the best thing is to leave yourself loose and decide your path through the storm.

In Gaurav's case, life could not have been more surprising. By a stroke of luck, as he would now call it, he landed in another city, much bigger than his small town. His father somehow managed to send him to Hyderabad, which was one of the urban centres in India. Being a megacity, there were all kinds of top-notch education and career opportunities in the city. Like all traditional parents, Gaurav's mom and dad wanted to see their son becoming an educated gentleman. To make it happen, they were willing to spend the last penny in their pockets.

Gaurav knew his parents wanted a promising career for their son. Seeing their dedication, he complied with everything they asked him for. At the age of twenty-two, with some teaching experience, some business experience, and lots of big dreams in his eyes, Gaurav stepped on the Hyderabad train station. The city welcomed him with its typical hustly-bustly demeanour that Gaurav was alien to.

His small-town eyes were beginning to absorb the busy city life on the one hand. On the other, he could not get rid of the afterthoughts of his business downfall. "Maybe I could revive it if I get one more chance." "If only I get to keep my business, I could make so much money in a few months' time" was all that was going on in his mind. Somehow, the train of thoughts in his head did not align with the externality of the changed lifestyle and goals in this new city.

As they say, time is the best healer. Gaurav got accustomed to his new routine here and adopted his parents' goals for the time being until, of course, he bumped into another opportunity. As unexpected as this move was, there was some silver living for Gaurav to get going with it. One of the best things about coming to Hyderabad was that he was all alone and by himself. Here, he could explore life in greater depth without anybody telling him what to do and what not to do all through the day.

Gaurav had completed a bachelor's degree in accounting from his hometown. Now, he was going to pursue further studies in the same field. In Hyderabad, he joined a coaching centre for Finance and Accounting. The plan was that he'd do further studies here and get a job in the relevant area and make his parents proud. For him, the first and foremost thing was to become financially independent as soon as he possibly could.

In Hyderabad, a lot of students came from other cities across India in hopes of a brighter career. There were numerous hostels that would provide cheap accommodation to these aspiring youth. Gaurav, too, lived in one such hostel. His accommodation was an average building, not very comfortable either. Here, four boys would share a single room with only enough space for a single bed for each.

The boys sharing the room could not have a night of super comfortable sleep if it weren't for their hectic schedule. Every morning they would wake up to a queue for the bathroom. One toilet catered to no less than twenty people. So, the rush was pretty much justified.

On the other hand, the Hyderabadi food wasn't the best for Gaurav's stomach. Back in his town, he would consume entirely different food. His mother would cook all the meals for the family herself. Here, Gaurav had to consume hostel food for the most part. The city had its own cuisine. There were episodes of stomach upsets in the beginning, but eventually, everything settled down as Gaurav's stomach adapted to the city's taste buds.

When all of the settling down in the city was taking place, Gaurav was complacent for being on his own. Walking along the streets of Hyderabad, he could smell freedom in the strong gusts of wind. It was as if the trees were reminding him that he was not bound in this new place.

As much as he missed his family, he was ecstatic at the prospects of leading an independent life. There would be no restrictions on Gaurav now. He could do whatever he wanted to. The thought was consoling.

Perhaps that or the urge to explore the new place or the excitement of making new friends or the natural instinct to survive or all of those things combined sped up the adjustment period for Gaurav. It didn't take him very long to adapt to city life. In just a few months, he knew every nook and corner of the city.

In the first few months, Gaurav had coaching classes late afternoon. So most of the time before the classes was spent preparing or studying for them. In between, he would munch on his regular meals, which were never grand or special. After the classes, however, he would roam around the city and explore the unchartered territories. He would visit places he had heard of and also pay a visit to some of the most mundane places. After all, his aim was to get acquainted with the city. This way, Gaurav memorised the entire city's map in his head. You could name a lane, and Gaurav would guide you the way in no time.

Gaurav wanted to travel extensively, but he was constrained by the finances. Small pocket versus big dreams was a constant contradiction in Gaurav's life. The annoyance he felt while peeking inside his pockets before making any plans had not stopped bothering him. Hence, somewhere inside his heart, he still dreamt of making lots of money with which he would afford the lifestyle he had always longed for.

The huge coaching centre for finance opened a new world before Gaurav. On his first day, he heard some people talking in fluent English and could not help glancing in their direction, only to shift his gaze back to where it was for fear of making a spectacle of himself just moments later. The interpersonal skills, strong communication, high self-esteem and self-confidence were things Gaurav admired the most in his classmates. He quickly made a couple of, in fact many, friends at the academy. After spending some time with them, he realised he was quite far behind the others. They had the skills and personality Gaurav lacked. However, the qualities his friends had were not impossible for Gaurav to acquire once he had set his mind to it.

Out of all those things he aspired for, excellent English speaking skills seemed the most important to Gaurav. In his head, he was thinking, "I'll be more confident if I can speak flawless English like my friends do. I'll also sound more attractive and feel more self-assured." Hence, "Forget about accounting; it's time I improve my English speaking skills, or I'd be far behind those my age here" was Gaurav's last resolve.

It was not that Gaurav had never studied English at the school. He was from a family that knew the value this language held for children of the day. So, they entered Gaurav in an English medium school where all the subjects were taught in English. The problem was that at the school, they didn't get the students to talk in English as much. So, conversing in this language became an ordeal for people like Gaurav. Every time he spoke English, he found himself struggling with the right form of verb, correct article, or the perfect use of tense for the context at hand. That did reduce his confidence as the others were speaking as if English were their native language, and Gaurav felt a little primitive in comparison to them.

In a bid to be like his friends, Gaurav took admission into a language training centre. It was a private academy that charged people some money and trained them to speak better English. They would offer English speaking sessions to the students, mostly in the evening. Most of these were aimed at helping the students get a job at different positions, such as call-centre representatives, receptionists, personal secretaries, and other desk jobs at various companies.

In other words, these institutions would train the young lot for jobs in the highly competitive market of the growing Indian economy. Gaurav came here to improve his language skills and thoroughly enjoyed the experience. Here, they would employ different types of teaching methods, with a greater emphasis on oratory skills. There would be confidence booster exercises. The students were asked to speak before a class of about 50 people, interact with their respective group members and discuss things among themselves. They would give presentations on different topics and practice communication widely.

The focus of the training was teaching the intricacies of the language and getting the students to practice them. The addition of physical cues and some fun activities here and there made the training all the more interesting. For Gaurav, these classes were the best parts of his day. Every morning, he looked forward to attending them. Learning fluent English was a process for sure, and Gaurav was enjoying this process immensely.

He was one of the fastest learners at the coaching centre. He soon became one of the best students in the entire class. His instructors acknowledged his efforts and were amazed at his progress. One day, he was at the language centre when one of the members of the administration approached him. "Hey, the instructor is ill. He might not come for a long time." "Oh! Is that why we had a free period today? I see." "Yes, now we need somebody to take his position and continue the batch. We were just wondering if you could give some time to this place. Would help you, would help us as well."

The offer presented Gaurav with an opportunity. He was enjoying studying at the language coaching, but teaching English to others was a different thing altogether. He was not adept at the language. On the other hand, he thought he could upgrade his skills by teaching others and making some money on the side. Prior life lessons also rang louder in his ears, "Grab the opportunity when it shows up. Don't waste it." So, he agreed to take the position after giving it a serious thought.

Gaurav was right. Teaching English to the students improved his English like nothing did. With this new role, Gaurav's routine became busier. He would take accounting classes, filled with technical concepts, in the afternoon. Later, he would go to the coaching and refresh his lessons before the class. The latter was much more refreshing and exciting for Gaurav.

Most of Gaurav's days revolved around work. He didn't know anyone in this city apart from one person from the same town who used to live miles away from his hostel. The new friendships at the coaching were still in the formative phase. There was not much hanging out in the beginning except for occasional visits here and there. He had also grown very fond of the girl who used to work in the office of the coaching centre. Now that he was one of the instructors, he had more time to talk to her, and there was an infatuation. He was really enjoying this time in Hyderabad as all this was very new to him, his work with the coaching centre continued for the next six months.

One day, Gaurav was winding up the class at the language centre when one of his students approached him. He told Gaurav that he had an interview that evening for a position in one of the multinational companies. The two engaged soon engaged in a conversation. The boy asked Gaurav, "Would you mind accompanying me to the office? I actually need to perform really well to kill the interview. I feel if I'd have someone to practise my speaking with along the way just before the interview, I could do really well." Gaurav loved to be of help to people, and he was free that evening anyway. So, he didn't take much longer to agree.

The two boys got into the car and headed off to the bank. It was located in one of the poshest areas of Hyderabad. As the car entered the vicinity, Gaurav noticed some of the finest buildings he had ever seen. He couldn't take his eyes off the tall, glassy exterior of the high rise constructions. Every one of them had strict surveillance outside the building.

They parked the car in the parking lot, which was expansive. Brand new cars shone from afar. The sleek bodies of those studded across the area attracted Gaurav's attention. He caught a close glimpse of them before entering the building after multiple security checks. The building was much bigger on the inside than it looked from the outside.

They walked to the reception. The lady there asked them to wait while pointing at the room across the end of the hall. They waited on the mahogany sofa set with an elegant table in the middle for a few minutes. A representative from the Human Resource department entered in a while to take them to the interview hall.

There were going to be open interviews. A number of aspiring candidates sat across the hall. The boy informed Gaurav that the panel would take anywhere between four to six interviews before selecting the final candidates, so there was going to be tough competition. Another man from HR came and gave them each an extensive form to fill. While Gaurav was only there to support his student, he asked him to fill out the form and try his luck, and Gaurav did so.

By a stroke of luck, Gaurav applied for the position and cleared the initial screening. One by one, he cleared all the stages and was only left with the final interview before the panel. His student, unfortunately, failed to get through and was disqualified at some stage. Gaurav felt really lucky. However, he realised how inappropriately dressed he was when he glanced in the direction of the other candidates.

They were all dressed immaculately from head to toe, with their beard properly trimmed and their hair combed backwards in a gentlemanly fashion.

Gaurav, on the other hand, was in his routine shirt and a pair of jeans. Neither did he have proper shoes, nor did he look presentable enough for the interview. He had dressed up for a class and not for an interview before leaving the hostel after all. He was asked to change into formal clothes for the final interview. He did request the staff to conduct his interview some other day, but they plainly refused, saying, "All the interviews are going to be conducted this evening. We won't be having any further interviews after this. So, if you really want this job, go back home and come here dressed up nicely."

Now, Gaurav had to go back to the hostel, change and come back. He was excited but was without any preparation. He barely knew interview etiquette. He wasn't sure if he really wanted this job in the first place. Gaurav got to the hostel and, along the way, made up his mind to avail this opportunity. He thought he was getting little money from coaching, and his expenses were skyrocketing. He had a new friend's circle he wanted to hang out with, and he needed money to keep up with them and meet his growing expenses.

By the time Gaurav got to his room, he was convinced that he needed this job. It was strange how he decided to appear in an interview and got this close to getting a good job in a split second. He learned some quick etiquettes from a friend and went off to the interview. Outside the interview room, he sat on the couch, waiting impatiently for his call. He looked here and there in anxiousness. In his mind, he was revising some of the bookish things he had studied in his academic life.

Gaurav did not know what the panel would ask him. It could be something from his academic background or something he had studied at the coaching. They could also ask questions related to teaching and gauge his personality through his answers. It was uncertain and exciting at the same time. Unaware of how the environment inside the interview room would be, Gaurav was framing all the wildest scenarios in his mind and making strategies to evade them.

Gaurav got some time to practice. He did prepare answers to some of the questions that popped up in his head. When his turn finally came, and he was led into the room, he was a bit nervous, but he covered it up with the way he talked. He did stumble a couple of times, but his communication skills and confidence helped him regain his composure. He had been working on his personality really hard, and that came in handy in dealing with the interview questions. By the end of the interview, Gaurav managed to impress the interviewers, who seemed clearly happy with his performance.

On his way back to the hostel, Gaurav was thrilled as if he had come back from a daring adventure. Appearing in an interview for one of the biggest companies in the country in a matter of hours and killing it at the same time was no less an achievement. Gaurav took the opportunity and employed the skills he had learned to cast a good impression.

On the same evening, he received a call from the company and viola! He had got the job. The HR person told him he would be given a monthly salary of Rs. 10,000, and the news sent chills down Gaurav's spine. The amount was equivalent to about 100 pounds in today's time, but it was still a lot of money for him back then. Gaurav was elated at the thought of working in a multinational company and making good money.

Just when he was celebrating the news, Gaurav remembered he had other commitments. He had to make a decision. He could take this job and compromise his studies, or he could focus on his studies and forgo this opportunity. The decision was a difficult one, as he knew that he did not do very well in his studies in the end, neither could he sustain his business, so any decision would need agreement from his parents and wider family. But Gaurav had already done business now, and there was a different attraction to actual work experience compared to studies. Also, he was under no illusion that he was still studying in a very ordinary institute (compared to top business schools), and nothing was guaranteed in the future from a job perspective. So in his mind, he knew his decision. He was always more interested in gaining real-time experience by physically working at some place than acquiring bookish knowledge. So, he decided to take this opportunity. He would go to consolidated weekend sessions for his studies and attend the new office on the weekdays. This way, he could also continue language training and make some extra money by doing two jobs at a time.

Gaurav was in-touch in with his parents all this time. However, he chose not to disclose everything to them since, being conventional parents, they wouldn't approve his plans. On a call with his parents, he told them that he got a job at a multinational company and that it was a part-time thing. Just as he wanted, his mom and dad did not create a fuss about him getting a job. Gaurav's parents wanted him to pursue further studies and get a degree. They would never agree to him working in the city where he had only been for 7 to 8 months and compromising his studies.

Getting a job felt like the best thing in life at that time for Gaurav. He was really focused on his new job. The office he worked in was colossal. The office was a combination of open plan and individual compartments for the employees to work separately. The architecture was more towards the modern side with a top-notch interior. They had well-trained staff at the office for the smallest of jobs. Gaurav was super excited to be working here. This place had so much to offer in terms of grooming and learning that Gaurav wouldn't trade this opportunity for anything in the world.

Gaurav was deeply enjoying this new chapter of his life. He was working in a multinational for the first time in his life. By this time, his personality greatly improved. The big dreams he had seen at some point in the past had started materialising one by one. This job was the beginning of an adventurous ride. Gaurav was going to experience much more in his new workplace.

Chapter 6: Pathway to Success and Changes

The new job and the change in his life made Gaurav enthusiastic. The ambience of huge offices like data centres made him feel amazing. The typing and talking skills are the essential things to learn in the training period. One of the first training that he went through was to decide what kind of job he wanted to get within the data centres. The organization would give four weeks of induction and training, depending on your scores and progress. He was good at most written tests, but he could not succeed in his voice and speaking skills.

He was unable to get a job in any of the voice based roles. Some blessings are blessings in disguise, as he was not offered the position in voicing, so he was transferred to another field. Every person has their expertise, and Gaurav was good at data analysis and typing. He was isolated from the group and transferred to the data processing instead of the calling team. At that time, the worth of the data processing team was lesser.

As the voicing and calling department was better, the pay scale offered to the employees was also more. In his case, however, Gaurav was happy with what he was offered. He joined the data processing team and was quite pleased with the decision. During his work, he could see other employees

68

stressing out, but this was the first proper office experience for him, so there was more excitement than stress. As Gaurav was not fortunate enough to have a proper college life, this work atmosphere where many employees were of similar age to Gaurav felt like a college experience.

The workload was less as compared to the other department. He used to do what he was asked to do by the manager. He used to get training for whatever the work he was offered. It is true about what people say about happiness. It is reflected in whatever work a person performs. The same was the case with Gaurav. His joy was reflected in his work. He was never stressed about the workload. Over a few months, his attitude towards work got his manager's attention, and he could see that his manager started to trust him with a number of activities which usually would be done by more experienced members of the team.

The relation he had established with his manager over time was not something planned. Neither was he doing something to impress the manager or to get closer to him. It was just that he got more engaged with the work rather than complaining about work. But the people around him assumed something else, and the picture was shaped according to the people's negative perspectives.

When the manager was shifted to another job, he offered Gaurav his position. The team comprised of eleven to twelve people. The team had many senior people, they were all older than Gaurav, and some were married with kids.

His situation was interesting as initially nobody in the team ever thought of him as their manager. It was difficult for him to be the manager even after being selected for the role by getting the interview. The position was undoubtedly challenging, but he was convinced that he will be able to do the required job.

Gaurav simply got on with the job and asked his team members to do the same. He knew that most of the team members had many complaints about the previous manager and the situation will not be any different for him. He understood the fact that there will always be problems where ever you go. Whatever the position you are given, people will always find ways to mock you.

Sometimes challenging, but the time at work proved to be really good for Gaurav, he was also blessed with meeting the love of his life, Natasha. She was in the same office as Gaurav. He achieved things back to back, starting off by getting a job, meeting his girlfriend, and getting a promotion.

After spending eighteen months in the organisation, Gaurav was finally bestowed with an opportunity to go to Hong Kong for a project. At that time, any chance to go abroad to work with an organisation or work with a client directly was considered the best thing you could achieve in data processing centres. You wish to pursue plans, but fate has other ways of doing things for you, just like Gaurav, who could not grasp this opportunity because he did not have a passport at that time. Until last year, Hyderabad was the largest city he had seen. Never in his wildest dreams had he thought of such an opportunity to go abroad. This particular opportunity was not worth missing out on specially as this was offered to him without any competition, but he could not take the offer due to his passport situation. This affected his impression in the office because he turned down the offer, which meant that there would be more options like these, and he would not be considered for such positions again. These thoughts made him take immediate action. He got his documentation sorted out and every other possible thing needed for such processes.

At the same time, his girlfriend also got an opportunity to come to the UK for about three months on a project. She was extremely excited as she was ambitious as well and knew that opportunities like these could potentially change your life. He was very happy for her and at the same extremely sad that she would be away for three months. This was the first time they were going to be apart for a long period of time since they started dating. Her being away in many ways brought them much closer as now they used to talk for hours on the phone. As months passed by, the anticipation and excitement of her return increased, and she also felt the same. Upon her return, they celebrated like crazy and it was one of the enjoyable times in Hyderabad.

During this time, his relationship with his girlfriend evolved; there was no doubt about his immense love for her. The relationship was the same on both sides. The relationship went on well for a year, never had he ever thought about leaving her or about anyone else. They were working in the same office, so even work was fun and enjoyable for both of them. Sometimes he would think that most likely, he would be getting married to her. This was because this was the first time he was in a relationship, and he did not really know any other way. As they were both competitive at work and also used the work in the same department, he started to that there was starting to be a little comparison between them, especially where their work was common. Gaurav had an introverted nature, and he liked being the quiet one in the discussions as he used to enjoy observing things more than speaking.

Whereas his girlfriend was the opposite of what he was like in the office. She was the dominant one, always addressing people how things should be, sharing her thoughts. In the beginning, this didn't affect him; instead, it made him happy because he was madly in love with her. He started noticing how the same situation was making him uncomfortable now. He compared the time when he joined the office, how happy and relaxed he was but now, over time, he was changing as he never used to feel irritated before.

Every time Gaurav and his girlfriend had an argument, he felt awkward. He could not name the feelings and emotions he was experiencing at that moment. He realized that he was not enjoying the whole situation; he could not name the feeling specifically. This might be because of the subtle things in the relationship or the comparison with others. He thought he was doing all the things people do in relationships normally. He started to feel irritated and tired more than usual and noticed that his lifestyle had changed dramatically since he had been with this girlfriend.

One thing that was clear to him was that he did not have any resentment towards the situation. Everything felt laborious. It is the kind of feeling when you spend a lot of your energy arguing about certain things, but it still did not make Gaurav feel resentful. He was still sure about his love for some reason, and he knew he would only spend his life with her. He knew he would propose to her, and they would be together at some point in the future.

There are some times in your life when certain situations of present remind you of your childhood experiences. As the relationship was not going as smoothly as he would have liked to, Gaurav felt the same as he used to feel in his childhood. He started recalling those questions about what life was all about, money, relationships and society . Why were the things the way they are in reality? What was the reason? At that time, he ignored them, kept these questions unattended, giving mind logical reasons that they were just random 'thoughts'.

He began to reflect on how he could improve his relationship with his girlfriend or how to maintain that bond with her. He started to think about progressing more in the company and increasing his earnings so that they could have a comfortable lifestyle. He formed the plan in his mind. No matter how many times the unanswered questions would strike his mind, he would give them no importance and work towards his current goals. At last, he knew, or he thought he knew where his life was heading towards.

Chapter 7: Opportunities Knock At the Door

After the Hong Kong disappointment, Gaurav was not sure when or if any similar opportunities for projects abroad would ever come again. Gaurav made sure to get his passport, and other documentation was also done as soon as possible. Life has several ways to teach you lessons. This was also new learning for him, as he was just eighteen months old in the corporate sector and had to change his thinking from being a student to someone who wanted to create a career. His life in Hyderabad was all settled now. He was in a respectable job with good prospects, he had a girlfriend who he loved, and his family back in Rourkela were reasonably settled. His only ambition at the time was purely professional, and he was determined to grow within the organisation.

After about six months from this incident, Gaurav got an opportunity again. He got a chance to go to the United Kingdom (UK), which he dreamt about. Gaurav always had a special connection with the UK.

Gaurav, since his teenage years, had been a huge fan of cricket and football. Most people support their countries, but Gaurav had a deep connection with the game itself. He would watch test matches all the time on TV. His most favourite time was watching test cricket which was played in England. The main reason why it appealed to Gaurav was simply that it looked good, so picturesque. The surrounding seemed very green and fresh. People who are residing in England mostly do not like such kind of weather, and as a kid, he used to think if he would ever get an opportunity to go to the UK, he would watch cricket there.

In addition to that, he was also a Manchester United fan, which was considered the best team in England in the 90s, full of English national players. Then, Gaurav started to support English National Team. Upon revisiting the memories, Gaurav had a funny incident during the World Cups, Euros, and other national tournaments. All his friends would either support Brazil or Argentina if it was World Cup and Germany if it was Euros because people did not know much about the other teams. They would just by default support these countries, and Gaurav supported England as everyone in the UK knows how people usually get disappointed with the penalty loss. He knew that if he ever had the opportunity to go to the UK, one of the first things would be to go and watch live sports.

The idea of going to the UK was always at the back of Gaurav's mind. He, as a kid, visualised it many times that it would happen someday in real too. At that time, it was nothing more than a fantasy. Although people in the UK hated the weather, Gaurav loved the idea of a cold country, maybe because he was born and raised in India. India is usually hot in almost all ten months. Gaurav got the chance to stay in the UK for six weeks initially. He had to go through an interview process that was negotiated on his part.

Gaurav knew it was for six weeks, but at the back of his mind, he was always thinking of going there for an extended period and seeing if there were more opportunities for a longer duration. He did not wholly dwell on it and focused on enjoying his time and getting the project completed first. At that point in his life, he was already away from his family. So the only sad part about that trip was long goodbyes for his girlfriend. They both had the idea that it was just six weeks that would pass in no time.

Another reason that doubled his excitement was that this project was like promotion as he was expecting a raise in his salary. In addition, it would mean a lot for him because his salary was average back in India. Working in the corporate sector improved Gaurav's lifestyle. Comparatively, a better lifestyle meant spending all the money that he made. He needed a life-changing chance that would allow him to make extra wages to make more savings.

He started to ponder upon the idea of saving at that time because he knew his girlfriend, and they were both on the same page. They both knew they would work hard and save money. After a few years, they will eventually get married.

It was very typical for Gaurav to think about a settled, happy marriage at the age of twenty-seven, especially when you know you have been in a relationship for over a couple of years. Gaurav was not the only one to think about this idea, and his girlfriend was also the shareholder of the same thoughts. This is what they used to talk about – getting settled, having kids and much more.

At that present moment, he did not have the time to look back at his life. This was one of the most amazing things Gaurav was never sure of. He never used to get stressed or bothered about the past anymore, not even the day before. Sometimes when he used to talk to his parents, they would usually remind him about the business days and how miserable he was, but for some reason, he had totally forgotten about that and had no resentments or anger towards it, just remembered the lessons. That helped him maintain the momentum and continuously work towards his goals. Above everything, he started looking forward positively. He never used to overthink about the situations or let the negativity take over him. His first reaction would always be positive. He did use to ponder this question often, that why is his default reaction to even the worst situation positive. He could not understand it as it felt like an unconscious habit.

Gaurav was very acutely aware of the people around him in his family and friends circle who used to complain a lot and also thought that he was naïve to be positive all the time. Gaurav was never very keen to be around such people as it used to put him in a negative frame of mind. Rather than looking at the brighter side, people would always criticise. Gaurav did not do this by thinking about positivity all the time, or he believed he always had to be positive; it was just that the positivity was already there in him.

When he discussed the opportunity to go to the UK with his family, the overwhelming response was excitement, but at the same time, they were scared as he would be going out of the country. Gaurav found it fascinating that people were more worried about what he was going to eat in the UK compared to being excited about the work opportunity. It's not that there is something wrong with thinking about his food and physical wellbeing, but at that time, he was not concerned about these types of things. These things were secondary for Gaurav because his primary focus was on himself and growing as a person meeting new challenges in life. He was thrilled for the adventure he had yet to experience rather than worrying about what to eat. He remembers how he used to think about this as an exciting chance to go to a new country and meet new people.

Till that time, Gaurav always trusted his positive instinct. Regardless of the reason why. But he knows he has been naïve previously as his business ended up on the wrong side.

However, he somehow managed to forget about the time and still looked forward with positivity. Gaurav often said to himself how lucky he was in life. Even though he had many unfavourable situations throughout his life, there was always this feeling that he was still extremely fortunate.

He did not think this way for the cause of fancy thinking, but he just used to think he was lucky without knowing the answer of whys and buts. After a few weeks, Gaurav arrived in London with a team of six people, including his manager and four other colleagues who were at the same level as Gaurav. He remembers how he bought only one suit in Hyderabad just before leaving for London. Everyone was told that they were all going to be at the head office in London. Most people wear standard attire that is a suit and tie. He had never worn a suit before. He never really owned a suit back because he never needed one. This is one of the most common practices of middle-class men, and they do not buy anything unless it is required. The same was the case with Gaurav.

The suit reminded Gaurav about the time when he needed a suit for a wedding when he was younger and borrowed the suit from one of his friends. He admitted no one should ever wear a suit in India because of the hot weather. Refreshing the memories from the past, Gaurav landed in London, which was his first-ever long flight and second-ever flight of his life. He was enjoying all the new experiences. It was November when they all came to London. He remembers coming out of Heathrow and going out for a smoke after a twelve-hour long flight.

As soon as Gaurav came out, he could not ever forget the moment when he took his first breath. It was so fresh, crisp and chill. It was a bit cold, but with that subtle happiness of landing in London, the weather was not a problem. It was incredible because the atmosphere was how exactly he imagined, with shade, no sun and cloudy with a hint of chilly winds. The group took a taxi to Canary Wharf from the airport, a place in London. The place was like a financial and corporate hub in London. They all arrived at the serviced accommodation and stayed at a serviced apartment.

The manager had all the members set, the manager had a separate room, whereas all the other people were divided into an apartment. Two of the people shared an apartment with two beds, each with two people staying. Another thing that Gaurav noticed was how empty the streets were as compared to India. It is human nature when they leave a place and go to the new one, unintentionally comparing both places. The same was the case with Gaurav. He unconsciously related the streets of India no matter how big or small the town or city is; streets are always busy. And here, he could see the vast differences.

As soon as Gaurav entered Canary Wharf, it seemed like he had entered an inhabitant place. Gaurav noticed that it was not the weather or chilly wind that took my attention; he loved that place's quietness, peace, and tranquillity. The serviced apartment was beautiful. Looking over a marina, wherever your sand boats are parked, it looked picturesque. The scene was so perfect that it looked like a painting. Everyone kept their luggage and got fresh. The first thing that all the colleagues did was to get a drink. This was the first trip of Gaurav, but some of his colleagues came here for the second time.

Everyone got out immediately and explored what was outside. Gaurav and his group landed there on Saturday and had Sunday off before the working chaos began from Monday. Gaurav was very excited to explore London. After informing his family and girlfriend about the safe travel, he forgot everything. The allowance according to that time was not high, it was around twenty pounds a day. For those six weeks, Gaurav spent all his allowance. He knew saving the allowance and not enjoying the UK would be a very stupid idea.

The next working day, which was the first day in the Canary Wharf office, was similar to when he joined the office in Hyderabad. He was totally in awe of the sorroundings, infrastructure, professionalism of how people were dressed, how they communicated and the view from the 40th floor of his building overlooking the city of London.

Chapter 8: Exposure and Comfort

The time Gaurav was spending in the UK was memorable. Despite all the new adventures, he was living in the moment to get an overwhelming tour experience. One of the primary reasons that made Gaurav happy was the financial stability he got at that particular time. He was so relaxed that he did not think for a second about the challenges he might have to face at work. Sometimes it is not the things that make you exhausted but the circumstances. As Gaurav was mentally invigorated, the challenges did not seem to drain him out mentally and physically. Gaurav, along with his colleagues, did the usual touring in London.

Sometimes when you know you are at a place you have been dreaming about, and that too for a limited time, you try to take in all the moments altogether. You want to explore every little corner of the place, which happened with Gaurav and his colleagues. Along with his team, he saw London Bridge, Westminster, Madame Tussauds, and other places tourists go. They had unforgettable moments and had fun together in the first four or five weeks because the days felt like holidays. At least for Gaurav because those days brought happiness for him.

It is not that the office work was not hectic, but the eight hours' long shift did not affect his excitement. Every day at the end of office hours, he had the same energy and excitement he felt at the beginning of the day. Therefore, he ended up spending all his allowance.

Some of Gaurav's colleagues were a bit conservative as they had a different approach to having fun and money. They believed in saving money which is understandable from their perspective. They had young families to look after and responsibilities to manage. This was a good opportunity for people like them to save money. His colleagues had already done short-term projects in the UK., so they had an idea about where to spend the money and how much to save from it. The other factor in favour of Gaurav was the weather. It was the chilly nights and cold weather of the UK that made him fall in love with that place over and over again. The thing Gaurav liked about winters was the opportunity to wear suits, overcoats and gloves. Walking into the office wearing a suit with an overcoat gave him a very professional look that felt appealing to him.

People love wearing such a wardrobe if they never had a proper chance to wear it before, for instance, people living in India. Gaurav definitely enjoyed taking advantage of this opportunity. Some of his colleagues did not like winters which more or less made them incapacitated during the whole season. However, waking up in the morning was equally tiresome for Gaurav, too. It is often a constant struggle for working people to get up early in the morning regardless of the weather.

Winters just make mornings lazier. Gaurav knew that the rest of the day would be fine despite all the struggles once he was out and about. The good thing about winters is that you do not feel hot and sweaty all the time. But for the sake of complaining, Gaurav complained about the weather sometimes like everyone else; otherwise, he was comparatively fine with it. Sometimes you have to follow the people just for the sake of fitting in with the group and getting along with each other.

It is not that his colleagues were exaggerating it. It is true about UK's winters. Whether it is a local person living in the UK or a foreigner, they would always end up complaining about the weather at least a few times a day after checking it. Gaurav never had the habit of checking the weather update ever in India. However, in the UK, he also adopted the habit of checking the weather every day, just like everyone around him did.

The starting five weeks went by very quickly. The last week in London was before Christmas break, and that was early in December. Gaurav's manager called everyone in his apartment for an announcement. They went in with mixed feelings of nervousness and surprise, for they were expecting an update on the project but were unsure what it would be.

There were some rumours about the extension, but nobody was entirely sure about the news.

Everyone had the idea that they were most likely needed here for another four months. That was absolutely amazing for Gaurav because he enjoyed being there. Not only him, but his colleagues were also in the same boat as well. Everyone was excited about the longer stay because it was a great opportunity to stay there and make an impression. Making an everlasting impression was more than anything because it also opened the door for more money. As Gaurav used to get a handsome allowance, it was sufficient for his living expenses during the six weeks, and then incoming four months, he knew his salary in India was getting accumulated savings which were beneficial for him in many ways.

It was rewarding for him in a way that he was already planning to save for the future. He used to talk to his parents and family once a week, but he managed to take time out for his girlfriend because they were sharing the same company. Gaurav and his girlfriend used internet messaging to talk about how things were going. They kept talking just to keep each other updated. He used to miss her a lot, but his main focus was staying in the UK for a long time, making progress in his career, and saving money for the future. He wanted to save money not for himself but for both of them and their future. This was one of the factors that kept him motivated throughout the time.

He had a couple of great colleagues he deeply respected and treated like older brothers as they were more experienced than him. So he never felt alone, especially in the first few months in the UK. The extension was final, and they were given the opportunity to go back to India during the Christmas holidays for a couple of weeks and then come back again for the first end of the first week or second week of January. Gaurav went back to Hyderabad – he did not have enough time to go back home to meet his parents – but he went to meet his girlfriend and had a blast with his friends.

Gaurav and his girlfriend were both excited as things had started to work in their favour. It was indeed a blessing to have the love of his life and money together simultaneously. Life felt smooth. Gaurav had the idea of what the future held for him, but the easiest way to explain would be, at that point in time, whatever he had, his future was kind of a new adventure but with the same people in his life. Gaurav and his girlfriend used to wonder what it would feel like to stay there for a few years rather than just a few months that felt amazing to imagine. After that, they were planning to get married, and she would come over, spend a few years in the UK with him, travel across Europe, and eventually go back to India and settle down.

Anyway, Gaurav came back to London in a couple of weeks; this time, he was more goal-oriented and focused on work. He wanted to see how he could turn the situation in his favour and get a longer contract. As usual, he did not have any cunning plan or shortcuts, so he decided to give all his attention to work, enjoy and see what happens later on. At this present moment, his mind was already playing tricks with him. Although he knew that time in London was limited, he started to see himself living here long term. If you want to get things done in UK or London, you would simply have to follow the process, unlike in India where you have to be cunningly smart to bribe someone to do something stupid or play a shortcut to get your work done. Gaurav was never good at doing work through shortcuts.

Gaurav was convinced that he was made for this country. It was peaceful, and for the first time ever, he realised following a proper process works. Weather it is the small things like queuing up for a train or a complex visa process. One of the other things that Gaurav loved about the UK and London, in general, was how people know to really enjoy themselves in life. He loved going out because of the atmosphere. It was something else. Specifically, the West End in London because it was just not you going to the pubs, bars and restaurants, but it was the vibe in the city.

Gaurav had the experience of going to music festivals, clubs and a list of entertainment was just endless and boundless. He often used to tell his girlfriend when they used to talk on the phone that he should definitely do something and ensure that he was here for a long time, and then she could come and join him because they both knew there was no way they could ever get a similar lifestyle back in India even if their salaries raise to double the amount. It was the freedom Gaurav craved for that he got here. However, the entertainment and limitless ways of entertaining oneself also attracted Gaurav.

It was the simplicity and professionalism that made Gaurav fall in love. He was impressed by the simplicity, how everyone would work through a proper channel and follow the set standards to get a task done. It is not just to get the work done but, generally in life, how professional everyone was. At least, that is how things looked like from the surface for Gaurav.

This also made Gaurav reflect upon himself and realise that he was still lacking somewhere and needed to work on his personality, interpersonal skills, and technical knowledge to improve himself and get a chance to stand out. By doing this, his chances of staying in the UK will increase, which was the driving force that motivated him. At the same time, Gaurav, for some reason like previously, used to think he was lucky. He has always been fortunate. He would never rule out any possibility and see how life turns over.

Chapter 9: Meeting New People

Being in the UK for about six months – the actual time of the project that Gaurav came for – he was very keen to stay there for an extended period. He was not entirely sure about his current project, but somewhere in his mind, he knew that he would want to live there forever if he had the chance to. There was no doubt in his mind that he was meant to be there. It did not matter how much he missed family or his girlfriend and friends. He had been lucky somehow to even land in the UK. There was no denying the fact that he could not just let this all go away without trying to do his best to continue his stay.

Gaurav never lacked motivation since he started his business. As a teenager, he was very motivated, but this was something else. A year ago, he would not have even thought about coming to the UK, let alone staying there. The thought of him being totally disheartened after the business collapse and debts came to mind, and it felt like in a blink of an eye, he was in London planning his future. A few years back, he thought that he would be doing business and never really move out of Rourkela, his home town.

As he was working in London, one clear thing was how cosmopolitan the city was. When he was growing up, he always wondered if all foreigners, people mainly from Europe and America, were the same. In his mind, he had no idea how many different styles of cultures existed, different food, ways of living, and thinking.

In a way, it was very liberating. He was a person who, as an Indian, was supposed to be restricted and who had his future all planned out in his mind, which was essentially acceptable by the society – especially the society he belonged to. He had a weird thought one day; he thought he must expand his company more and make it more diverse. He enjoyed the first six, eight months in the UK with his colleagues who came with him from India. But he noticed that they used to do nothing different from what they used to do in India. They ate the same food, dressed the same, watched the same Bollywood movies, discussed similar topics and participated in the same activities. The only difference was the location. He decided he would expand his friend circle by meeting locals in London irrespective of where they were from rather than only Indians. This will be the only way he will be able to experience something different. His colleagues who came along with him to the UK left after spending six months, and his visa got extended for another six months. He had to spend that time alone, and he absolutely had no issues with that. He did feel bad because he and his colleagues who came over from his office in India were close. Gaurav used to treat them like his elder brothers.

It felt bad to see them go while he was staying back alone. However, he was also happy that out of all others, he got an opportunity to stay for an extended period. This made him even more determined to try and stay in the UK for as long as he could. He had no proper plans to impress people at work apart from just taking responsibility for work and being easy to work with. He could not think of any other way of making sure that his work was recognised, resulting in another opportunity to stay in the UK.

At the same time, he was enjoying his work and his newfound lifestyle. The freedom he had now came with being alone. Gaurav made some terrific friends at work. They were all from different ethnicities. Some of them were from South Africa, Australia, New Zealand, some were Indians who were very different because they were born in the UK and a friend from the Caribbean who had been in the UK since he was ten years old.

Also, by now, he was much more integrated with people he had met locally. Gaurav used to live on his own. He was so absorbed in his work that he had no time, and whenever he used to get some free time, he enjoyed London, and the culture and lifestyle attracted him mainly because it was liberal. It would not be wrong to term it as inclusive, at least with the people he had met. He used to love the fact that things were very professional at work as well. He kept his professional life and enjoyment apart from each other.

Gaurav was twenty-five years old, single in London, with a decent job at that time. The freedom had started to have an impact on his thought process. Suddenly he strongly felt that there was so much more to life than what he knew and what he thought. He started to feel that he had not even lived properly yet. Gaurav had many conclusions in his mind about how life should be and used to think he knew his direction of life and what he wanted from it. This was a very funny feeling, as it somehow crept into Gaurav's mind and made him doubt himself.

He was too busy to dwell on this thought. He moved on with this busy life. He liked the scheduled days, going to the office and routine tasks. He used to work with very nice people who were kind and helpful, at least to his face they were all good. He very rarely felt homesick. Gaurav used to think that if he was good to others and everybody around him, the other side would be the same. It was a strong feeling in him, not knowing the reason, but it was just like that.

Talking about the workplace, things were going well. Gaurav had to work on himself to get better as the work environment was very competitive. Given that he was in such awe in the first year to be just in the UK, he just learned a lot by just watching and being observant. He used to enjoy talking to many of the senior people at work just because he wanted to see what type of mindset successful people in the corporate sector have. At that time, of course, a managing director in his company would look very successful person to him. He felt that learning was much easier if you had a keen observation, primarily because most work scenarios are mainly managed by handling the situation better rather than a pass or fail like we used to have in school.

Gaurav used to go out for drinks with a number of his senior colleagues, and a few of them were very nice to him and would always ask him to join as well. It is not that they would ask him; they used to ask everybody around to join for a drink after work. He noticed that it was such a great way to know people, especially seniors, and to understand their expectations from you at work rather than trying to do it all by yourself without understanding what was necessary for the team and management. On the other side, he used to talk to his girlfriend almost every day, and he used to text a lot as well, so they mostly stayed in touch. But for him, it was tough to have a long-distance relationship. They started to feel like they were just convincing each other to stay together and hoping that the plan would work out in the next couple of years.

Gaurav had the option of getting married once he got settled and bringing his girlfriend over to the UK. However, at that time, they only had plans about focusing on career. Gaurav was trying to extend his visa, and once it was done for a substantial period of time, it would be the right time to settle. He was fine with the plan, but deep down, he knew that he was postponing things. He thought that there was so much for him to see and do, and he could not do all that without freedom. At the same time, Gaurav travelled a bit across Europe, Amsterdam, Belgium, Paris, and Munich with his friends, who were also locals. That was the first taste of a proper holiday for him as he never had a proper holiday throughout his entire childhood or teenage life.

Gaurav knew he had so much to do, and he loved his girlfriend a lot. It was evident that he would not break her heart. They used to video chat on weekends, but being in different time zones was also an issue. They both wanted the same thing, but they started to drift apart a little bit. After spending the first year in the UK, when the project was close to its final stage, he asked one of his managers if he could get a chance to stay in the UK for a more extended period as he loved it. He was unsure what they would think of me, but at least he maintained a relationship where he knew that he could at least ask them the question.

To his surprise, his manager informed him about his extension for another two and a half years the next day. They were expecting him to move to a permanent role if Gaurav wishes to take it and stay here. He was excited. He knew this was going according to what he planned. Now he could see a day where he could potentially spend four or five years in the UK, become a citizen and stay permanently. Gaurav did not tell his parents initially, as they thought he would only stay for a couple of years. But in the long run, stay in India because they did not want him to stay for too much longer in the UK. Gaurav's parents would never think about this, leaving his homeland and then suddenly not returning to India permanently after that. During this time, Dhruv was finishing his higher education. Dhruv was great support for him as he did not have to worry about his parents constantly; his brother was there to take care of them when needed. By this time, he took full responsibility for his family. Gaurav's father still worked, but it was not a consistent income. Gaurav used to send a sufficient amount to cover all the costs and his brother's education whenever required.

Chapter 10: Struggling with Life and Love

Although he had the financial side sorted and had a decent salary in the UK, Gaurav was still worried about his relationship as it was his future. He loved the time he spent in the UK in general. He was busy exploring different cities, for example, Scotland and Wales. He also met various people simultaneously and slowly noticed how his mind was changing with time. He remembered when he was in India during his teenage years and believed in God and religion, which he suddenly realised that he hadn't thought much about it since he had been in the UK.

When he was coming to the UK, he forgot about these concepts. His new surroundings led him to see things from a different perspective. He saw how people used to live a much more organised life and work. He started to think that there was no God or anything similar to this concept. Religion was human-based and had no real existence apart from people's beliefs, and as long as he would try to aim for bigger things and eventually achieve them.

As life was going on a smooth track, he was not bothered at all. He just thought success depends on how hard you work and for how long. He used to work long hours and felt responsible for the job in hand. Sometimes he tried to impress the management because he had also learnt some corporate tricks staying in the industry but completing the job always remained his focus. His performance at work remained consistently good, he was highly rated, and that was quite clear from when he used to get his appraisals.

When work was at its peak, it became harder to stay in regular touch with his girlfriend. She came to the UK to meet him, which was indeed a wonderful time. He met her after about several months. They had a amazing time as they travelled across the UK, Scotland, and Wales and also a great time in London. But, he also soon realised that it was time for her to go back in two weeks.

At that time, he seriously thought if he was making the right decision by not asking her to get married immediately when his visa had been extended for two years. But he was not entirely sure what she was thinking either. For some reason, he could not ask at that time, mainly because there were doubts due to his change of mindset and having a slightly different outlook on life. He had many things to look forward to. At the same time, Gaurav knew that getting married right now would stop several things he wanted to do on his own.

Staying in the UK, he noticed that being in their thirties and not being settled with family was prevalent. People were in happy relationships but not married. However, if he wanted to get married at around twenty-eight in India, no one would be surprised. Still, it would be considered a little late. It was challenging for him to see her go off to India after two weeks of holiday. Then again, after being sad for a few days, he got back to his routine.

As always, Gaurav's life was busy. He was going back to his normal self-engaging with life, but also, at the same time, he knew he had to make a decision. The risk of losing his girlfriend for good as he started to feel that they were slowly becoming apart as a long-distance relationship over the phone was no longer going great. They usually ended up in some argument. That was chiefly because he could feel she could not be a part of his personal life anymore.

Gaurav could sense that her friend circle had changed, and she was busy with work as well. It was a difficult period for both of them. At some level, they both understood he was not ready to be committed to a relationship and have a family right now. Which sometimes made him think she should move on from him. She wanted to have a family and a settled life. After all, there was pressure from her family as well to get married. They both eventually broke up due to their arguments and misunderstandings.

At the same time, Gaurav felt sad. This was probably the first time he was upset to such an extent. He couldn't remember if he had shed a tear in his entire childhood or even in his teen years. What he considered essential to him at that time somehow had fallen apart. After this incident, he was slightly lost as he was not wholly sure again about love and life in general. He used to ask himself if love really exists the way he thought about it or was this nothing more than just the hangover of watching too many Hollywood or Bollywood movies. He wasn't even sure if true love really meant anything.

The breakup was significant. However, he did quite well because he only felt the pain for a few months. This was a long time for him if he thinks about it now. On the flip side, he started to feel good within a few months because he did not have to constantly worry about calling somebody or checking and continually trying to please someone. This is what he used to do when they were together in a relationship. However, he was sad initially but started to feel better. He also started to get over slowly and focused on his work by keeping himself busy. During this time, he used to stay alone and given that Gaurav was single again he thought he should now utilise his free time to upskill.

He started going to gym classes, took a few Spanish and French lessons. This was not just to get away from loneliness but also to get himself upskilled. This also allowed him to meet more new people. His work slowly started to get impacted by his personal situation but he continued to push on with his willpower. Sometimes it got hard for Gaurav to push himself when you are not entirely motivated constantly. Due to the stress, he had this feeling of not performing well at work in the UK, but going back to a job in India at that stage was out of the question in his mind.

Gaurav's primary goal was to make sure that he could stay there for at least five years to ensure that he had become a citizen there as getting a British passport would make it very easy for him to travel around the world. He loved everything about the UK. This country gave him the opportunity to a new life, expanded his mind, and showed him how to enjoy life in many ways he could have never imagined in India. Gaurav was still a little confused. At this point, he knew his life was exemplary, personal life was not so great, but it was not stuck in one phase. There was a void that could not be filled no matter what. He used to think that this was because he had now started to miss his family.

Gaurav felt these emotions strongly because he used to spend half of his day thinking about his girlfriend. He had been spending much time thinking and planning the future together. When they were not doing this, there was a considerable gap. It was an unsettling feeling. Gaurav was surprised to see that he used to spend so much time overthinking and planning only. One day out of nowhere, he thought to himself that there has to be something more to life than this.

He thought that you struggle and work hard. You take everything joyfully, but that does not mean the result is in your favour. Why do you want to achieve so many things when you know that it is stressful and emotionally painful at some times? He somehow had this belief that this cannot be all of life, job, girlfriend, getting married, having kids, and them retiring one day. Gaurav was somehow convinced that there was more to life, but people around him had no answer to this.

Chapter 11: Stay and Poles Away

Gaurav had been in London for a few years now. There had been significant incidents in his life by this time, but he was still relaxed and joyful. He knew he had many questions about the bigger picture, but at the same time, he was confident that he knew his short term plans. Although he thought he had become more serious about life and future than ever, the primary driver was fear of failure. He was afraid that he would squander this great opportunity that life has presented to be in one of the largest cities in the world and work in a multinational where he could create his own future. Gaurav was living the life he had always wanted to live. He moved on despite having regrets about the breakup.

Now that he was single again, Gaurav had moved in with a couple of guys in a penthouse in London where he used to work. He stuck to his original plan of meeting more local people, so he decided to live with some local guys rather than finding Indian flatmates. One of his roommates was from up north near Manchester, and one was from Eastern Europe, although he had lived and studied in Atlanta. He had a great time with all of them. Gaurav had the best time of his life; he used to go out for dinners and movie nights and had a lot of fun with all of them. The fun was not limited to partying alone but sports activities, gym and odd trips across Europe.

While living in the UK, Gaurav was introduced to many new things. One of the most surprising ones was how little he knew about Hollywood cinema. As growing up in India, he mainly knew Bollywood (the Indian film industry) apart from the basic blockbuster movies of Hollywood like Jurassic Park, James Bond, Star Wars and Indiana Jones etc. He had no idea how ignorant he was on so many different aspects of life. Gaurav was surprised as he felt that TV cinema helped him expand his mind to another level. It was an enjoyable experience for him. At the same time, he thought to himself, why do most people always think they know everything about life when in reality it's impossible to know even 0.1% of what exists at a given point in time, forget history.

Occasionally, Gaurav had flashbacks about his breakup, and then he would think about his ex-girlfriend even more. He had this unsettling thought in his mind that he was doing all this stuff to distract himelf from not missing her. At this time, Gaurav was uncertain about his feelings as he was trying to hold on to some of the memories because no matter what, he was still fond of the time he had spent with his ex-girlfriend. Gaurav thought that he was going to start dating again. After about a year of his breakup, he felt a lot freer. Along with his freedom, there were many more opportunities and chances for him to explore.

Gaurav experimented with a lot of things like travelling, meeting new people, but he was clear that he did not want to be in any kind of relationship. The lifestyle he had adopted gave him many chances of hook-ups. Such relationships failed to last longer as they spurred the moment kind of thing. He never managed to enjoy these relationships for too long as he felt like taking advantage of someone that he could not be committed to.

Gaurav was also unsure about the feelings that come with such relationships. It is in human nature to feel bad about things that disappoint you. It is normal to feel this way if the love relationship you thought would last a lifetime only last for months. Gaurav felt like people take such relationships for granted. He knew that if he were not ready for the commitment, it would be wrong to take advantage of someone else. He sometimes thought maybe he was the one thinking in such a way about relationships. But, in the end, it was not a problem; at least he knew he had moved on. Gaurav was committed for a short period, but such relationships were never serious from both sides. The relationships followed similar phases, initial days were always perfect, but Gaurav could not force himself to do things that he did not like genuinely. He was undoubtedly caring and loving, but these two traits were not enough for the long-term commitment. So Gaurav gave himself multiple reasons why the relationships never worked every time.

Gaurav used to go to India once a year to visit his hometown and meet his family. He had a different life in India around his parents, friends, and siblings. He had gained a lot of popularity in his hometown, especially after living in the UK for a few years now. He had noticed how the behaviour of people towards him changed. Everyone was keen to meet him more than before. Generally, Gaurav's family had always been good to him personally. Apart from that time, when Gaurav was doing business, he lost money, and he did not score as well in school exams as he could have. Otherwise, he had always been treated well and liked by all the family members, including his relatives. During these visits to India, he made many great memories, especially when he attended his friend's wedding. As Gaurav came back after a long time, he met all his old school friends that felt great.

During his stay in India, Gaurav noticed something unusual about himself. He observed that whenever he met anyone close to him, whether his friends or family members, he felt like he had just seen them yesterday. It did not matter after how long they met, and he always felt the same thing. There was not a single day when Gaurav had missed them. It sounds weird, but that was the current mental stage of

Gaurav. He never missed anyone. It was just like when people are around you, you remember them, but you do not miss them once they disappear. He never missed his friends, and maybe this is why he felt like he had just met them yesterday. It was a strange feeling for Gaurav as well because when you normally meet people, they would say things like, 'Oh, it was nice to meet you after a long time and so on, but he failed to feel it that way.

Apart from India, Gaurav had also travelled to many countries across Europe, Middle East Asia and some of the cities of America by now, and he had loved every single bit of those trips. He used to spend all his money and save less due his lifestyle. He had been in the UK for three years, but still, he was not sure about his long term stay in the UK. He wanted to travel to as many places as possible from London before his project ended in the UK. At this point, he had no idea that he would stay in the UK for another eighteen months to ensure he qualified for citizenship, as it depended on his company to extend his contract. His performance in office was going strong, and he finally got a further extension for two years which took his time in the UK for five years. He realized that he was extremely lucky and grateful for the company and the people in his management team that made everything possible. Gaurav's performance played a part, but he was very aware that there are many talented people around, and you need some luck to get these decisions in your favour. These things would have never been possible without the hard work and help from the people around you. Gaurav was very close to fulfilling his dream of getting UK citizenship.

Gaurav was sure about making his dream turn into a reality, but he knew he would not take any action to jeopardise this achievement. He knew that everything was going smoothly, but deep down, he had the feeling that something was missing. For some reason, he felt that this was not enough; he was unsure about himself. He knew that the lifestyle he adopted was to distract himself from his chaotic mind, but yet again, he felt something was not right. He always felt something was lacking in life, but he had no idea about what that 'something' was. Sometimes Gaurav felt that the only solution to this problem was finding a girlfriend and trying his luck again with a good, lovable relationship. He thought that the only way to be fulfilled again was to get in a relationship and have a family.

Gaurav has never been on social media previously, and he knew that he needs to get a profile online if he needs to start dating again. Gaurav never preferred to be on the phone or laptop after spending working hours in front of the screen. Gaurav never had any social media presence. He never completed any social media forms that were required for an account. But as he had decided to date again, the easiest way to find someone was to register and set up a dating profile on him on all the dating websites. While creating his dating profile, he came through an unusual realisation. The profile asked him about his hobbies, preferences, and dislikes. He realised that he had never focused on his personality. He used to think that strong personalities looked great on TV or movies, but it was a very stressful and stringent way to live in real life. At the same time, he liked that he had an adaptable and flexible personality.

To sum up this, Gaurav was unable to create his dating profile as some of the questions were left, which made him realise that he was limiting himself to only a few things, and was it really true that he was these few lines that can be updated on a form. It was a funny realization. He realized that it would be even worse that he would be judging people based on similar information which is available about them. Gaurav was never a kind of a person who would like to judge or pass a judgment. He had never passed any judgment because he understood that you never know enough about people to pass a judgment. At the same time, he also knew that judgment was required and needed to fit in the society or workplace, but not required to meet someone new. Gaurav was unable to complete the form at that time. He decided that he would meet someone outside at work or social gatherings, or on his travels. Gaurav rejected the idea of putting himself through the process of selecting and judging someone by a written form of data. Gaurav believed that filling a form was a great way of recruiting people for jobs as people's skills can be defined but a limited approach to finding love or someone worthy of relationships. The fundamental characteristics and human traits can never be defined but can only be experienced over time. Unlike the people of that age, Gaurav used to think this way but never shared his thoughts with anyone. He kept his thoughts to himself because he feared that people might not understand him. They would probably consider Gaurav stupid, but it was the reality that could not be changed.

At the same time, Gaurav had to face a lot of pressure from his family and relatives to get married. He kept on delaying the matter by saying he was not ready at that moment. Deep down, Gaurav's romantic nature compelled him to dream of finding his partner in the most unexpected ways. One can say he impacted watching too many movies, but he did not lose any sleep over it.

After some years, his flatmates had moved on for various reasons; some left for a relationship, while others left for work purposes. At this time, Gaurav decided to live on his again. He could not find someone to move in with him immediately. As he realized that he had now achieved some of the goals that he set about when he came to the UK, he would feel happy and always acknowledge that he was very fortunate. But no matter what he had thought he had achieved or wherever he went, this constant feeling of lack and emptiness followed him everywhere. The rollercoaster of feelings made him question the concept of life, in general. He wondered, what was life all about? Was it just earning and working hard? Or was there something else to achieve?

Gaurav was bored of his work life, and the work became monotonous and boring for him. He had been doing this for a few years, and it was getting repetitive.

He was still conscious and careful about his work mainly because of the fear of failure that kept him going through this phase. It is a phase of life when you want life to take new turns and experience new things. Humans often long for a change when they are frustrated with carrying the same thing for too long. Like you cannot hold a glass for a longer time, the same way you cannot carry a monotonous routine for too long. Gaurav used all his willpower to push through life, but the motivation just went below each passing day.

There was no doubt of fun and entertainment in his life, but he was bored of that entertainment as well. It seemed like everything he had was not enough for him. Gaurav recalled a particular event where he was talking to a friend about his state. Gaurav shared his genuine concern that he is not excited about doing anything anymore. When he is in a gathering, he will enjoy and have fun, but as soon as it ends, the excitement is gone. He used to wonder about the same things when he was a child. What was life all about? When he was a kid, going to school, it looked like grownups knew and had everything. It excited him greatly and he was keen to feel adulthood. Now that Gaurav was thirty years old, he still had the same feelings and questions. Now he had experienced more things than he ever expected in his life but still felt empty, just like how he felt as a child.

Narrating his experiences as a story felt good when talking to people about what you have done so far. But this also felt like all his so-called achievements are only relevant in comparison to someone else. One key take that Gaurav had learned already was people and things in life come and go: the more you run after things, the more they go away from you. As he realized that throughout his life that he can remember, from starting in school, or starting work or coming to the UK, he has been setting targets, always thinking one day, it will stop, but targets keep moving. The more money he earned, the more he spent, but there was still the feeling of lack. He knew it was time for him to upskill himself to find a new direction in his career.

Chapter 12: The Down Time and the Hollow Inside

There are times when you feel that no matter how hard you try, you cannot get out of the disarray that your life has become. The same happened to Gaurav as well. There were times in the UK when he felt like he was completely alone and could not get his spirits up.

When Gaurav was in a certain environment, he would be fully involved and enjoy himself, but that excitement could not last beyond that point, as in one time out of there. He had the same question again that he used to have as a kid. What was life all about? When he was a kid, he thought that adults do not go to school because it looked like grown-ups knew everything. When he was thirty years old, he had done relatively well for himself, but he still felt like all this was past and had no meaning at all.

It was a feeling that anything he knew about himself was only in comparison to some other people in the world, but at the same time, it felt like he does not know anything about life. Everything Gaurav was experiencing was a temporary feeling. It was hard for him to obtain a constant sense of peace in his mind. He felt like he was losing his sanity in this chaos. The more you chase something, the more it goes ahead of you; it is a fact of nature. He had this thought many times that this activity would be the end of the goal, but it always expanded further and further.

Gaurav went through difficult phases and faced everything with strong willpower. This phase frustrated Gaurav, but on the surface level, he composed himself well as he remained calm, joyful, never got angry with anyone around him, and had no resentments. He was unusual because he understood one trick from life: being relaxed and calm can help deal with other people around him in any situation. All these incidents and feelings were very personal as he still felt hollow as if something unique and profound was missing in its true essence on the surface level.

In between everything, something strange happened with Gaurav. It had an incredible impact on his mind, body, and generally on him. Gaurav was unsure if it was the outcome of one single situation or a combination of different incidents or experiences, but he had an unexplainable unique feeling. One night while returning from a party, he felt a high-pitched noise that passed through his ears, as if it was tuned into some radiofrequency. This feeling stayed for quite a while when he walked towards home, and he could not hear anything outside apart from the high pitch noise.

After a few minutes (not exactly sure how long), he felt this unusual quietness, which was unexplainable. Usually, even if you are in a quiet place, at least your mind constantly chatters and talks. At this moment, there were no thoughts in his mind that it was a confusing situation, maybe it was the noise that stopped his mind, or it was something else. Gaurav was unable to comprehend this situation and his feelings at that time. In hindsight, Gaurav noticed that something truly changed in him, but at that time, he could not explain what was happening. As he could not understand the situation, he thought to himself, was he losing his sanity or maybe 'out of his mind'?

After all this, there would be several occasions when he would be at home, and his mind would go extremely quiet. For Gaurav, quiet meant that there would not be much chatter or self-talk. In his mind, this situation was peculiar and confusing because he had never experienced this situation before as he only knew his mind when it was thinking or chattering. It was a situation when you do not think that there is even a possibility that the mind can be quiet of self-talk. The feeling is impossible to explain, as you need think in your mind to explain something.

Initially, Gaurav was confused, but at the same time, he began to ponder upon his thoughts vividly. Typically whenever a thought came to his mind, he would follow it up by an action, reaction, or judging the thought or by thinking if it is good or bad, or condemning the thought or feeling happy. These were usual reactions to the thoughts that occurred in his mind. But now, suddenly, he would just observe his thought without any reaction. This was a very confusing state.

Gaurav was not sure about his thoughts anymore, and he was unsure if what he was going through was really happening. He would usually try to distract his mind by watching TV or talking to people, and spending time at work was another way to himself divert away from this feeling. However, one noticeable thing was that he could detect his thoughts very early and felt that he had time to react to his thoughts, whereas, previously, he would not think about what he used to think. For Gaurav, everything inside him was happening for a reason, and it felt as if it was going in slow motion. For someone watching from outside, his reaction would look spontaneous, but to him, it felt like slow motion. This went over a few months, and to his surprise, suddenly, his judgment was suspended.

There was a sense of happiness because there were no judgments. Gaurav would judge in terms of what he wanted to eat and how he would talk to people but deep inside, it was not a severe issue for him anymore. Gaurav used his force and willpower to ensure that everything was going on in his head had no impact on his work. To his surprise, this was not necessarily a bad thing at work. If you looked from the upper surface, Gaurav looked like a calm person around at work, and his reactions to something at work were standard as well. In general life, he started becoming very calm and composed, which was an appreciable thing.

This change was not just noticed by Gaurav but also by many other people around him. These moments started to increase, his interest in understanding his mind had also increased a lot. Gaurav had this strong feeling that something amazing was going on in our minds we hadn't really paid any attention to. At this time, he wanted to do further experiments with his mind. He was starting to enjoy the game with his own mind slowly. Initially, everything felt weird, but now he was enjoying the feeling of being quiet and observing his thought pattern. This would primarily include thoughts and feelings. On one fine morning, Gaurav woke up and suddenly felt incredibly quiet. It was a unique experience because he would linger a bit in the bed, but this time he suddenly jumped out of bed straight, went to his balcony; the sun had just risen, and he thought he was able to look directly to it.

Gaurav had never seen the sun like that before, he used to live next to River Thames and looked at the river as well, and it never looked so pleasing and brighter. Gaurav was stunned for a few seconds, but then he went back and wondered without fully understanding what that was in real. During this time, Gaurav's work was at its peak as he was swamped. He was working for his promotion as well. Gaurav forgot about all these things and went on with his routine work. Gaurav was the kind of person who had always been in a good mood, but he started to notice that his mind was much quieter nowadays compared to before. He had stopped commenting on everything like before, for instance, judging the weather, being angered by the crowd in the train, complaining about people or issues at work, which would be his normal surroundings because he heard all around the day.

This feeling was unique as before, and he would be judgmental or mainly annoyed with himself. Gaurav had this sense of knowing that his own thoughts react to these external situations and accordingly comments whether it's about good or bad, and the mind keeps doing this automatically for most things, unless we are consciously thinking about something or busy with something. There was a distinct quietness in his mind that helped him to see and understand his thoughts more clearly now. Gaurav knew that all these assumptions about his mind were his own, but he had to develop an explanation for what he was experiencing.

His parents and family members were keen for him to get married as he was thirty years old now. Working in the UK had helped Gaurav financially as he used to take care of his parents from the living expenses to medical expenses. By this time, Gaurav's brother had also found a job as he was starting his career. The only advice he gave to his brother was to leave his hometown as soon as he could and go to a big city. He said this so that he goes out and faces the challenges with a positive and confident mindset. That was the only thing he really knew worked. His brother was able to find multiple jobs in Delhi within being there for eighteen months. His parents used to set Gaurav with girls to get married, given that he was now a British citizen. Gaurav's mother used to mention several families interested in talking to them about the daughter's proposals for him. Gaurav was going through an incredible period at this time: work was frantic, his mind had infinite questions about life, and he was experimenting with his mind, which he did not start by choice. It just happened. He was excited and knew that getting married was not something he was ready for right now.

It was a fantastic time, and there was no way Gaurav wanted to drop all this by getting married. He was convinced that something was going on and could not just keep distracting himself and run away from it. At this time, he used to convince his parents that he was doing fine and they should stop worrying about him. He used his career as an excuse to get them off his back while he could continue carrying on with the experiments with his mind. At the same time, he continued to go on occasional vacations, whenever he got an opportunity and enjoy himself to the fullest. He has been planning a big holiday with his friends which involved a trip to Hong Kong, Osaka, Hiroshima, Tokyo and then back to London. This trip was going to be incredible as they were going to four different cities in Asia and specially the three Japanese cities that he has never been to. At the same time, the holiday would be a very expensive one as well. This holiday included a trip to the Formula One and knock out game at the Rugby World Cup. He knew that this holiday would be a great opportunity to take a break from work and day to day routine and have some time away to think about what was going on in his life.

Gaurav returned from Japan after two and a half weeks. It was an incredible holiday and time flew by which meant he had a great time. He had some funny incidents and some great learning moments which included losing his wallet in Tokyo. But even more importantly, he had some amazing flashbacks of his grandfather and memories of his childhood which he had totally forgotten but played very important role in shaping his adult life. He had no idea why this happened, was it because he was in Japan or it was simply just the timing of it. He felt much more relaxed and had a renewed energy since he's been back. Although none of his so-called life problems have resolved themselves. Gaurav continued to do experiments with his mind whenever possible, but he needed this renewed energy. He liked poking it till he could conclude something of it, which always felt odd since he was basically experimenting on his brain using his brain, further using it to conclude his thoughts and findings. The only reason he was not always playing around with it in an organised, experimental fashion was that he had work to go to as well. Work was always a relatively packed and busy schedule. And because of that stress and strain, He would accumulate over the day. He would usually be out after work, either to grab a bite (because god bless the people who still have the energy to fix themselves after being entirely drained of it at the end of a full-day shift) or to go out for a drink with his friends.

So usually, he would have about a few hours each day late in the evening to be on his own. Being left alone with one's thoughts immediately after tirelessly serving the corporate sector seems a little unsafe. Who knows what part of the trauma, disappointment, and emotional pain from work his brain might start processing all over again. However, this alone time was for relaxation, recharging, and re-energising mentally and emotionally, and that could only be television time, so there was not much going on at that time for Gaurav's experimentation that he liked doing so much.

However, as days passed, Gaurav found that he looked forward to spending time alone with his thoughts rather than avoiding them till he was recharged and relaxed enough to encounter them. He had a recurring question in his mind that now held a significant spot in his chambers of important and retained thoughts. The question was what actually was happening inside his head as he grew more aware of himself. As his physical and mental self-awareness grew, he could feel the initial question poising more questions rather than reaching an adequate and simple answer for it.

Usually, when he would fall asleep, he would notice right as he snoozed off, or even remember throughout the entire period of sleep when exactly along his line of thought he fell asleep. He started noticing this becoming a pattern, where he would tease his mind and explore his brain philosophically, only to expectedly fall asleep at some point along with that stream of questions and thoughts. He seemed to retain the remembrance, which is explicitly what bothered him for the rest of the day until he could come back to his bed and test it out again.

Most people do not notice or remember when they usually fall asleep or what they were exactly thinking at the time they fell asleep. The occasional times that they do is perhaps when they are on medications or are under the influence of alcohol. But Gaurav was neither, especially not every day, as he had a full-time job. He started to notice that he was mostly thinking about the same things every night.

Initially, it had been reassessing the day that had just gone by and what he had in plan for the next day or the following week.

Aside from assessing and examining his daily planner, the other things that occupied his head were the same personal worries, work-related events and issues, remembering random movie clips, or random other events, etc.

This realisation induced a unique feeling and state of mind for Gaurav. Previously, he would think a lot before bed. He had basically been doing that his life. But he did not know that he could see his thoughts rise and fall in his mind so distinctly as if he were staring right through a glass panel. It had a tremendous impact on him. Right as soon as he made this realisation, his focus on this unique state of mind began happening more consciously and effectively. It started to be a borderline superpower for Gaurav.

He possessed an odd ability to watch his thoughts clearly, and, as a consequence of this, his reaction to outside situations and stimuli became very composed and controlled. He was never really a hot-blooded, impulsive person by nature, to begin with. However, this change was something more fundamental than temper tantrums or bursts of excitement. It had more to do with how he now internalised situations, processed them mentally and ended up feeling about them. This change was almost robotic in nature, and it fascinated him as much as it freaked him out.

This new pattern of recognition and reaction to stimuli was not different from that of regular people. He noticed the fluctuation of emotion and back and forth between thoughts typical to a mortal mind significantly decreased. He observed odd, serene stability of some sort. As if time had been slowed down and fine-tuned somehow, but instead of time, it was his mind and heart. There were sometimes when he had almost no reaction at all. It felt like staring through robotic eyes, through which the connotation of emotion and irrational feeling had all been left at the other side of the lens.

Sometime after reaching this realisation, he remembered one of his friends commenting on how he would make a great poker player thanks to his poker face. Perhaps his friend had not noticed the poker face being a newer development but, regardless, considered it a strength, no doubt.

This showed the effects of this newfound realisation taking shape in his persona and character as well.

At some point, he enjoyed himself as these subtle changes slowly did homage to him and took shape within his character. He felt a tinge of humble superiority, not in terms of arrogance or ignorance, but rather in terms of his newfound ability for productivity and mental elevation. It was peaceful inside his head now. Even though he had not lost all emotions or feelings, he still functioned normally. Gaurav felt serenity and stability become a dominant environment in his mind. The peace, calm, and improved focus did not hinder his usual experiments with his mind but made them more productive and efficient. Now he really could experiment without previous interrupting factors.

Then, one night, just as he was about to sleep, he realised that he did not have many thoughts in his head. Normally around this time of his sleep cycle, his thoughts would feel like a heavily clouded sky, but that night it felt like the sparse, faded white cloud on a bright, clear sunny day. Despite the annotation of a clear sky, this feeling made him feel uneasy. It felt almost as if he were missing a part of himself.

However, it did not feel like a colossal calamity because it was not. It was a simple deviation from his usual night routine, which was fine for him. He came to understand how normal and acceptable this deviation was later.

Despite knowing that this situation was fine, he felt quite uncomfortable. He used to constantly think nonstop, and now the train tracks of his thought station were empty, the wind blowing leaves and dust bunnies across them.

He felt like he was falling into a deep, engulfing, dark well. Initially, he felt like he would hit the ground, but he kept falling into this large circular well, plunging into its depths. Then he noticed that a pot resembling a cauldron emerged from the side of the well's wall, similar to a step for him to grab onto. He caught it with both arms and held on to it. Just as he clung to the pot for dear life, it suddenly disappeared, and he was falling again. Then, like the first pot, a new step signifying a new thought in his head emerged. And then he hung on to that new thought for a bit, and he became that thought. Then it would eventually disappear.

This continued to go on endlessly that night until he fell asleep, slipping and sliding off scarce thoughts till a new one emerged. He could not even tell where he fell asleep during the train of his thoughts.

It seems like his superpower was gone.

He used to enjoy playing this game with his mind, and now it felt worse not having the ability to do so. This also brought a lot of confusion at the same time, as this was not how everyone around him thought about themselves. The thoughts themselves were fundamentally there in his mind. They were not arranging themselves in the natural manner that was familiar to his brain and its cognitive processes.

He began to question if his thoughts defined him at this point. He questioned why he felt so upset and how to process this sorrow and blankness he was new to. He hence plunged into an existential crisis that lasted several days. Gaurav had not "lost" his superpower per se, but in one night of its absence, he felt how much he had been missing his same old thoughts that define him. It felt like a break that he had not thought he needed. The kind he would put a 'much needed' hashtag next to, in a sweeping, insurgent tweet.

After several days, Gaurav reached a conclusion and epiphany regarding his existence. He concluded in his head that he was, in fact, not defined by thoughts. Because firstly, they are not tangible. Secondly, they cannot possibly be consistent and using something so random to define oneself seemed foolish.

He noticed how throughout the day his mind constantly judged people and situations, although these judgments were mostly positive from his side because he always wanted to create a friendly environment within and around him, he started noticing that his thoughts and feelings are actually the key drivers of how he felt about a situation. At that point, it was not so much the situation itself, or it was not so much if that the situation was good or bad, but it was the reaction to the situation internally. What he could theoretically conclude was that how one perceives the situation determines the reaction in turn.

He started to notice some subtle changes in him. In the real world, one's personality is the most important aspect of their existence. And he could not say to people that he was having doubts about his personality. It would shake the very crux of his existence, which had thus far been mostly built on the idea of intangible, random and feather-like thoughts.

He also could clearly see that his personality was nothing but what he used to think about himself. His personality was a complex amalgamation of feelings, thoughts, intellectual opinions, likes, dislikes, ideas, slogans, et cetera. This was incredible and relieving for him to acknowledge, and also frustrating

He realised the fact that, as a child grows to adulthood and the prime of his life, his physical existence, which is his body, is made entirely of the food he consumes. Gaurav felt similarly towards his brains, and it was as if he had been feeding his brain all those perceptual and intellectual thoughts that defined its existence and growth at each point in time, he also noticed that there is no fixed state of mind. This raised another question which was why we as human beings try to find an ideal state of mind when it does not exist in reality.

It was a shock in many ways, but he still doubted everything. He still wasn't sure what all this meant. So, at the same time, he would spend a lot of time at work, which was always busy, and his usual time off with friends. He knew that this was a way of distracting himself simply because just the feeling of not having a personality can be very fearful because one might not really know what they are doing and why. However, he did not really think much about this when he was around people.

This went on for a while with him until one day, when he realised that he did not really know who he was anymore. But the one thing he knew for sure was that he was alive and not these thoughts and feelings going through his mind. He was defined by something else, something more stable and intellectual. His thoughts had started to feel like clothing to his mind. Like clothes, you put them on and then discard them when you don't need them anymore.

So he could see that he existed as this 'quietness', for the lack of any words before any thought would arise in his mind, this showed him that thought 'tell me who I am' occurred, which was based on what others opinion of him. He saw no difference between what people thought about him or what he thought about himself because it was only an idea that he could create in his head to convince himself what he wanted to think about. But truly, Gaurav was something much more fundamental. And he was not just passing by a thought or a feeling trying to convince people what we should be. But he was fundamentally the power, the ability in which those thoughts arose.

So, the correct word was that he noticed that, without him, these thoughts and feelings would not exist. At the time, he used to kind of reference it to as the power of his choice. That he had this ability to choose which thoughts and feelings he wanted to give reality to. He could not ever see this before because he thought of himself as these thoughts and feelings. He had obliged every time when there was a thought in his mind and thereby assuming that he had no choice in certain life situations. We are the victim of this phenomenon we call life. This was an absolutely transformative feeling. But of course, it was not like thoughts and feelings had stopped inside him. He still felt normal, but he was slowly getting convinced that there was so much more to his life than what he had been taught and knew. He believed we limit ourselves to thinking that we are the content of our mind rather than knowing that we are the power that actually gives the mind the ability to function.

This did not mean that life was all clear to him. Some moments contemplating this was absolutely stunning and absolutely great. But it was still very confusing. Because he, at other times when he was working or was busy with something else, he would still think to himself, "Is this all real, or I'm just going out of my mind?"

Chapter 13: Mind and the Dependency in the World

The investigation in Gaurav's mind had become his obsession. It was by far the most complex and challenging activity that he thought an individual could do. Gaurav was not completely sure about what he was doing and what he was trying to achieve, but he felt like a pull towards it. All the other activities felt like a distraction. Gaurav was able to see his personality more clearly than ever before. He felt more like himself in such a way that scared him, but he also felt immensely competent. At the same time, he knew that he existed without constantly thinking about keeping up with his personality.

As he analysed deeply, he realised that everything in his mind was either the shape of thought, like words or images, like a combination of words, pictures, and feelings. Everything that he could be aware of by using his five senses was related to something outside of him, and this includes everything, from every person to object. He was the subject and everything else an object in his experience. All his thoughts were related to an object existing in this world and therefore was nothing original in his mind. He realized that any individual is capable of thinking about what exists, which means that the only unique thing about the individual is the context and not the content. It was like the inside was not different from the outside. In other words, transparent and easy to comprehend. In short, the inside was more or less similar to the outside.

At the same time, the unique thing Gaurav noticed was the ability to be aware of these things around. Gaurav was unable to explain it in words because it was not an objective thing. It was the subjectivity or the act of experiencing itself which is impossible to put into words. This was having tremendous implications on what he had been thinking all his life.

Gaurav could not keep thinking the same things when he knew that there was so much more to life, although his mind was sometimes tricked into thinking that this was nothing and we should enjoy life as we know it. Gaurav could feel there was much more to life, and it was nearly impossible to ignore. How could he be sure of any of this, he did not know, but he liked the fact that suddenly there was so much curiosity in him to know rather than constantly telling himself that he knows everything and what he wants to do in life.

He could see that he had been living and doing what everyone around him expected him to do. He felt that whatever he was doing was to please everyone and to be accepted. This does not mean that he had always been doing wrong, but he had never thought that the goals he had been aiming for were nothing but a reflection of typical society. It was interesting to realise that over ninety per cent of his time went by doing things for survival aspects of life. Gaurav used to think about getting to work primarily based on earning money to survive and live a better life. His life only revolved around a monotonous routine: eat, sleep, drink, work, TV, meet friends, wake up, and repeat.

These activities are great to keep a person entertained. Sometimes, he could not come to terms with the fact that life was limited to these things. This made Gaurav realise that he had lost that wonder about life he had as a kid. He wasted his precious childhood years and became a struggling and hardworking individual to deal with the problems that came his way, which he used to call life. But in the process lost his curiosity about life.

Whenever Gaurav felt overwhelmed, his attention used to go towards his breath and body. Something unique happened every time he experienced it. He noticed that his body was constantly breathing in and out with no assistance from him, which was essentially a bunch of thoughts. He realised he had been doing this every moment since he was born and had never stopped for a second since then. When the breathing stops, he will die. Gaurav knew about it already, but he had never thought about this, neither had he felt it so deeply before. He started to be mindful and focus on little details that he usually ignored before.

Gaurav noticed that his heart was beating and pumping blood to every corner of the body, which kept his brain working and allowed him to experience the world. This was an incredible thing for Gaurav. There is always so much going on in us every second that we never pay attention to it unless something is not working well.

Imagine for a moment that he had to run all these body systems by thinking and planning. It would be impossible, and he would die in two seconds. Sometimes this feeling made him humble because he had no control over any of these things. Gaurav knew that his body knew the truth and could understand life in a better way than his personality did. The human body knows that it cannot exist without the environment; the body knows that it is made of five elements: water, space, earth, air, and fire. It also knows that it will decompose one day and become a part of this earth. His body had no interest in what he thought about himself as the body regulates itself and goes about doing its job every second.

Although these things are natural and have been going on forever, they are also one of the most obvious things that none of us sits and thinks about. Gaurav could not believe he was never taught about these things in a certain way when they were school-going kids. This realisation opened Gaurav's mind to a new dimension of life that was more fundamental and real than what he perceived to be real before.

One fine day, Gaurav had pizza for lunch. While reading the backside of the pack, he noticed that ingredients were used from other countries. When the pizza arrived, he realised that the pizza he would eat would become a component of his body.

Gaurav had this weird thought that he had never had about food like that before. Since birth, he had been eating, but he had never looked at food with this perception. He realised what he consumed was made of what grows in the soil, and when humans die, it goes back where it came from. The body knows these processes very well and regulates accordingly, but the mind often has funny ideas. These insights into the body and its working were taught to Gaurav in school, but they were only introduced in a way to attempt an academic paper. Students were never taught these things to understand their implications and show life's oneness. The human body is a part of this earth, and it would not exist without this earth and its environment .

Suddenly the word 'ego' came to his mind. He has always heard this word from others around being used but never really understood the meaning of 'ego'. Within himself, he could never find it or point to it previously. He can now see that ego is nothing but like a shadow that can never be separated from a human being. Ego was like a character or mask within himself, which was a combination of his most repeated thoughts, feelings, likes and dislikes over his entire lifetime. This was made clear that 'ego' can be changed as it's not made of anything solid, but we are afraid to let go of the ego as it feels like nothing exists without it. But this was untrue in his experience as he could clearly sense that he exists even before the ego is born in his mind, which starts to take shape as we grow older and gets stronger as we repeat habits and fall into a pattern. Ego is a pattern that shapes our lives till we realize that it does not exist in reality and only as an idea in our mind, which can be changed. At the same time, he also realized that it is not easy to change likes and dislikes overnight as he has unconsciously practised them every day all his life.

Proceeding this thought, how could Gaurav think he was alone in this world and struggling with life? This insight into his mind made his life exciting. There was freshness and newness about everything with each passing day. Gaurav stopped using his memory to judge things all the time. The things might be the same, but the change in perception made everything new for Gaurav. He was well aware that nothing or no one had changed outside, but what changed was how he looked at them. There were still loads of challenges at work and personal life where he could see them as situations he would not like. Gaurav knew that he had to deal with the problems logically and more appropriately, but he could never solve any of them by overthinking and worrying.

At times, when Gaurav was worried, he could see that he was overthinking. He knew that worrying did not lead to solutions; instead, it absorbed all his energy. As Gaurav went deeper into it, he closely observed everything by focusing on minor details, especially when he was alone or in a quiet place. Gaurav started to notice a significant change in his daily routine and behaviour. He noticed he would repeat several things unconsciously during the entire day, mainly his habits.

The difference Gaurav observed was that he became self-aware about his actions, and some of his habits faded away as he could see that those habits had no value in his life. The significant difference Gaurav noticed was that he could differentiate better between healthy and unhealthy physical habits, but more importantly mental habits now. Indeed, it takes time to change habits, and it needs consistency and patience to break the cycle. The same thing happens when you want to quit a habit that takes time; at least you know the process of how it is working. Gaurav could see that his body did not need a lot of effort; he treated it with the basic needs without feeling weak.

For Gaurav, this was a great revelation and understanding. The respect for food and other things he consumed increased as he could see that the food he consumed nourishes his body. With this realisation, the unnecessary eating habits fell away and continue to do so. It felt weird when Gaurav compared the new pattern of thoughts with the previous one he once believed was normal. It was hard for Gaurav to share this phase and change with his friends. He could not discuss it with anyone. These thoughts made him understand things at a deeper level. He started to read more and more about matter and physics; and watched many videos and documentaries about various physicists and their work.

Gaurav was interested in physics because he believed it could teach him a deeper insight into matter-energy and the laws of the nature and universe. He had read physics when he was in school, so had basic knowledge about the subject. Gaurav was well-aware of some of the famous quotes from Einstein about how everything was one energy, how the entire universe was essentially one energy playing different forms. Gaurav was a colossal fan of Richard Feynman, known as the father of modern physics. He loved the way he explained physics in terms of nature and universe, which had nothing to do with complex formulas or theories.

One of Richard Feynman's lectures had a simple explanation of a tree, Gaurav had heard this before in school, but when he truly understood this, physics had a totally different meaning. He said about trees, 'People have looked at trees and they think it comes out of the ground that plants grow out of the ground, but if you ask where the substance comes from, you find out where does it come from.' The trees are a commodity here. Most of the substances come out of the air. The carbon dioxide in the air goes into the tree, and the change is it kicking out the oxygen and pushing the oxygen away. Water comes out of the ground, but it also comes from the air as it comes down from the sky. So, in fact, most of the tree almost all of the trees are out of the air. There's a little bit from the ground, some minerals, and so forth. How is it the tree is so smart is to manage to take the carbon dioxide to leave everything else? Some would say life has some mysterious force. It's the sunlight that comes down and knocks the oxygen away from the carbon. So it takes sunlight to get the plant to work. And so the sun all the time is doing the work of separating the oxygen away from the carbon. And the oxygen is some kind of byproduct which it spits back into the air and leaves the carbon and water and stuff to make the substance of the tree. When we take the substance of the tree and stick it in the fireplace, it makes an awful lot of activity while it's going back together again, and all this nice light and everything comes out, and everything

141

is being undone. You're going back from carbon and oxygen back to carbon dioxide and the light and heat that's coming out, and that's the light and heat of the sun that went in. So it's sort of stored sun that's coming out when you burn the tree'. This simple explanation is sufficient to show that life is interconnected at every level and is incredibly harmonious every moment. If this harmony breaks, nothing will exist. This also increased his understanding of the human mind and how it cannot be separated from the universe around us.

Our society makes us feel and believe that each one of us is alone and lonely in this world and separate objects which do not belong here. One thing was clear he may not be wanted by society or the people around him, but life will still remain in him and he would need no assistance from the people around him to make him feel part of this world. The laws of nature and the harmonious processes of our universe are happening every second of our lives, and it does not matter if or what we think about, thinking only impacts what we do as human beings, but we have no control or say over how nature works. The only way is to be in tune with life, rather than resisting it as we think we are a separate entity fighting for its own existence.

Gaurav was still unsure about how this scenario would link with religion because this was another topic that he had no real knowledge about its understanding. Gaurav's only expertise about religion was based on storytelling, which was based on the religious books related to all religions. All religions fascinated him as stories, but he was never really sure how something which happened thousands of years ago still impacted human beings so strongly. As a child, Gaurav had heard stories; the description and explanation of the universe from people like Einstein and Richard Feynman were extraordinary, but the same could be said of the religious books Gita or the Bible or the Quran. As he deeply investigated the workings of the mind, he could understand why some of the core messages from the holy books made sense, like 'Know Thyself', which essentially means understanding what we are first before taking any action as our identities define our actions. It made sense to him that the first thing he needed to know about himself was that he was not just merely his body, thoughts, or emotions. He understood that religion could be very contradictory as it was narrated thousands of years back and most likely was appropriate to the people who existed in those days. But the key understanding was not the events that took place in the story of the person in the religious books, but it was the context in which they dealt with the situations which made them special and different to others around them. There is no way we can follow the religion the same way today like it used to be. The human mind has evolved tremendously over the last thousand years, and every individual is capable of thinking logically, therefore religious stories sound like fantasies. But the lesson is not in the content of the stories but the context in which they were said. True religion; if that exists can only be practised internally. The outward displays are symbolic and have much less significance in reality. One thing was clear that he did not need to refer to a book to know how to behave in this world.

As he experienced his mind and the contents of his mind very clearly, he called all the 'known objects' as his mind but to see, feel and experience the phenomenon of life, he had to be 'out of his mind'. He has never ever been bored again as that state does not exist.

Chapter 14: The Greatest Discovery

Gaurav felt nostalgia when the flashbacks hit him. He could recall that when they were kids, they were taught to memorise many formulas in Physics, Chemistry and a lot of Mathematics. They had great learning of academic subjects but not enough knowledge of the implications of knowing that the whole world was a form of energy. This information gave Gaurav a better understanding of what he used to think about the world. Gaurav realised that his ignorance had led him to live his life in such a limited way. The new knowledge was expanding with each passing day.

Gaurav's knowledge expanded with day to day advanced insights. At this time, he still was unsure what his mind was before this new information. Gaurav felt overwhelmed; everything he had experienced in this period had made him look at the world from a different perspective. The five senses Gaurav could feel were unable to put in words the experience, let alone to prove it. However, modern science and neurology has already concluded that the human mind and the universe are interconnected. It is a bonding in which one cannot exist on its own as one is required for the other to happen.

Whenever Gaurav met emotional people outside with intense feelings and emotions, he felt more awake than others around him. He would see people reacting to situations in such dramatic ways that it would make him think he was maybe a bit more awake than them. Gaurav realised he could not stay conscious and be dramatic about a particular thing simultaneously. Indeed, life is not completely serious but harmonious. Gaurav wanted to enjoy life, but the most essential thing is subjectivity instead of objectivity.

Everything that Gaurav felt, the experience was inside of him; the only thing he had was the subjective feeling of that situation. Gaurav observed how fast things came and went by. For instance, when he was a kid, he used to get excited about toys. As he entered the next stage, the things that once made him feel internally changed with time. At that time, primarily outdoor games made him genuinely happy. When he reached the age of twenty, his priorities changed. The thing that satisfied Gaurav was earning money or having a good time. When he reached the age of thirty, money was his topmost priority. Apart from money, having his loved one and family around also made him happy. It was more subjective than the things that had changed outside, but the feelings inside him craved love. Humans crave love and compassion, which is subjective. He realized that the objects of desire have changed over the years but what has always been constant is the desire within. The desire has no colour or shape of its own, and our minds create it depending on the situations we are in at a given point in time.

Gaurav realised that his mind was an incredible storyteller. The mind saves everything that is perceived by five senses, whether the person is conscious or unconscious. Your mind records memories and gives you the ability to imagine the future.

The mind only narrates the situation as a story; Gaurav was convinced that he did not talk to anyone alone as he used to before. Gaurav had this feeling that he was speaking to someone inside him, but he could see that it was just a bunch of thoughts bouncing against each other in his head and trying to make sense out of it. It was mainly because there is always hesitancy in mind to be spontaneous. Gaurav wanted to be politically correct or have the proper knowledge to show someone that he was well-aware. To do that, Gaurav kept overthinking things in his mind while not realising that it was just one thought banging against another piece of thought inside his head with no positive purpose.

Gaurav realised that he had a choice of how he wanted to tell these stories and how he wanted to imagine the future. The most of stories he had told himself before were mainly to comfort him. If Gaurav were doing something naughty, he would tell himself a story about how it was a justified thing to do at that time, turning away the negative emotions. With this new thinking pattern, Gaurav observed that everyone thinks they are right because they behave similarly.

147

As Gaurav started to observe his mind, he could clearly see how everybody else's mind was working similarly because they were working on the same thinking principles and framework. Human minds work on the phenomenon that is constantly happening. He realised that he had never used his imagination properly before. Since the beginning, in his childhood, he had been given a certain level of education, mainly depending on where he was born. Gaurav's ambitions were set by the people around him, leaving him with no personal choice.

Gaurav chose to accept what he was being told to do even though he was very young at that time. Another reason could be that you think your elders know better and make the right decision. The advice was not always wrong. It was just that Gaurav was not aware of how much people around him influenced him. Even though he constantly tried to think that everything he did was original, most of his mind was filled with the same thoughts that came up most days, and he kept repeating the same actions.

Usually, it was a combination of eight to ten thoughts that surrounded his survival, entertainment, work, family and then he went back to the same thing again. Gaurav had never been able to notice this happening carefully before. For the first time, Gaurav could imagine a better future for himself. He realised that previously his future imagination was nothing but an exaggeration of his current circumstances, like a bigger house, more money, prettier wife and peaceful life. Gaurav knew that he had the right to imagine whatever he wanted to rather than projecting an exaggerated picture of today. The idea here should not be mistaken; Gaurav had the liberty to choose what he wanted to be rather than just being a mere person who had been pushed around by memories and present circumstances.

Gaurav thought, can there be anything more magical and incredible than the ability of imagination that humans have? He had no idea how to use it until now because it happens spontaneously. However, he could see that with a bit of concentration in his mind, he could set goals and imagine the things he wanted to achieve in life rather than just being pushed around by society, primarily existing thoughts and emotions that were limited to the past experiences only. By observing this, Gaurav could see what fundamentally was happening around the world with all human beings.

Some people do not understand that imagination serves as a tool that can be used to torture themselves with rather than thinking about harmonious things or human wellbeing. One night before going to bed, Gaurav was very relaxed and thought about the key activities for the following day. Suddenly, a thought popped into his head. The thought was, what if he died tonight and did not wake up tomorrow? It was one of the most incredible thoughts that took his attention. For a few seconds, Gaurav's mind could not process. It went all over the place. He got worried for a few seconds, thinking, *'Oh my God, there are many things to complete. What will happen, I have never really thought about this.'*

It was undoubtedly a scary thought. It was probably why most of the people never thought about it. By now, he had learned to deal with the thoughts in his mind and emotions within. Gaurav went deeper into this and realised that if he could not wake up again, there would be no one to know the consequences. If Gaurav did not have this body and mind and died, there would be nothing called experience. There would be no one to know, which was a massive relief in itself. He noticed that it was the thought itself who was scared rather than him. Yes, people around him will be impacted, but who knows, they may be happier without him.

Every night for a few weeks, he would go to sleep fully conscious, contemplating what would happen if he did not wake up the next day. He was shocked to find that every morning he woke up with a tremendous sense of fulfilment within himself which propelled him to now focus on things that really mattered to him in life. This would never come from outside because as we grow, desires evolve, but he was always trying to fulfil something by achieving or buying something. The fulfilment and joy he had always looked out for existed as though 'life' was already inside him, and he did not need outside support to complete himself. Gaurav's feelings of lack throughout were nothing but a thought created in his mind due to the ignorance of life.

He realised that beliefs are not required for our existence. This was another massive moment as all his life was simply driven by various beliefs about himself, life, work, others etc. He noticed that most of his beliefs were either picked up from a quote from a famous person, heard on TV or some book. It was shocking to see how misguided he was throughout. When we do not know about something, we simply believe, and on top of that, we think the belief is correct. The entire world is fighting about this, which is an extremely ignorant way of living as beliefs are not existential. Any belief can be created in our minds as that's what the mind does. It tells us to believe in something because we do not have a logical answer. As we live in capitalistic society, some common beliefs around how we structure our governments, financial systems, health and hygiene, for example, is understandable, but there is no requirement to believe in something to live. First, you exist, then you have the ability to think, then you believe. However, our current society is exactly the opposite which is just ignorance. We should be creating beliefs that positively impact human well-being as it's up to us to make them up, but most of the chaos and fight in this world to protect their beliefs which everyone should know is changeable on demand. As he understood this, there was no reason to behave with anyone or anything in a non-harmonious way as it's not required. This should not be misunderstood that we should not get angry or upset if people make mistakes or harm us, the reaction should be according to the situation, but keeping in mind that both sides have an argument and both believe that they are doing the right thing. Over 99% of his beliefs just dropped as they were useless slogans picked up from outside. His mind was now truly open and ready to accept or discuss things logically. As for our survival, logical thinking is mostly sufficient as it provides us with solutions for our problems. For things that he does not know, which is 99.99% of this universe as what he really knows in his mind is so small compared to the universe, he was happy to say 'I do not know' and therefore no beliefs. Believing and not believing about something or someone is exactly the same. Both are thoughts, and neither of them cannot give you the answer. The unique thing about 'I don't know' is that it makes him more curious about everything than ever before. Beliefs just make you think somehow that you know everything.

When he looks at every little moment of his life that he remembers, he realizes that every problem he has had was created by himself. There is no one else to blame as he made all the choices. Yes, some choices were demanded by external situations, but still, a choice had to be made. Funny enough that we never credit others for happiness but definitely blame others for failures. He realized that his mind was all over the place in the past. There were past memories of events, fearful imagination for the future, the constant worry of who is thinking what about him, how could he expect himself to make any other choices than what he did when the mind is in such a state. Now it's clear that the past has its importance in terms of lessons, so we do not repeat the mistakes but is not necessarily required to judge people all the time. Imagination can be used as it's required to clearly see what we want to achieve for ourselves if the necessary focus is applied. This can only be done when we are able to see the structure of our minds and our own identities.

He noticed that every thought or desire he had was selfish. Even if he was doing it for others, it was still to satisfy himself. Does that make him a bad person? Desire is a movement in the mind which is not necessarily about something, but it's the most basic instinct to live. If he did not have the desire to look after his body, then he would die. The same applies to all other aspects of living. The issue is never with the desire as we would not exist without it, but human beings have created this thing called selflessness, which is supposed to mean no desiring for ourselves. We

153

then try to achieve it, as selflessness never exists, no one can reach it, so they torture themselves and feel guilty about things. He realized that the only way was to be shellfish, but our selfishness has to be greater than us and include everyone around us. Then no selflessness is required in this world. Being good or bad has also been a dilemma, but our beliefs give us the confidence that we are always good. In reality, there is nothing good or bad on its own, it's had to be compared with something to be judged. Being good or bad depends on the situation and on perspective. Something which is good for him may be exactly the opposite for someone else. The key lesson for him was that every situation has good and bad, both included in it, but the way our minds work, we usually see one perspective that aligns with our way of thinking. It's the same as winning and losing, we may congratulate the winner, but there is no winner without a loser and vice versa as they are part of the same coin. Another law of nature that we have never grasped, this world is full opposites as there will be no north without the south or east without the west. For entertainment purposes, yes, we love winning and losing and all the drama, but in reality, it only exists in our minds. He used to think himself as a good person as generally he was nice to everybody around him, but now he can clearly see that he also made mistakes and took actions that adversely impacted others. So how can he say that he has always been a good person. He realized that to think good or bad about yourself constantly was probably the stupidest thing that someone can do to themselves.

One day he was walking along the river that is next to his house and suddenly looked up and realised that he was standing on a round planet which is ecological and self regulating, constantly revolving and spinning (never stopped since anyone was alive) around a huge ball of fire which never moves, then there are other planets and moons which are also moving at the same time in their orbits, and all this is floating in space which is infinite with no ground to fall on to. There are no directions in space. It's the same from every angle, there are no natural borders on earth, and there are no country labels on this world as it's all there in empty space as a whole. At the same time, all the activities of our environment and our bodies that keep us alive are simultaneously ongoing as well, and being stuck to the plant with some force called gravity. He had to sit down because this was magic beyond his perception. He thought to himself that he was so small in front of this huge cosmos at the same time what an incredible piece of the creation is a human being who has the mind and ability to experience this world by living. In fact, all life, from microorganisms to the largest forms, is incredible. All this together creates the environment where a species like a human being can exist.

The multiplicity of life is the beauty of life, all the divisions we have at every level from being part of a specific country, or religion or organization is created so that we have to live efficiently, but this should never be taken as fully true as these divisions are the cause of the world's miseries. All these divisions are in our mind, which then reflects outside as country, religion, work, relationship etc.

Our senses are so deceptive as well. For example, we always think that the sun rises and sets, but in reality, it never moves. This simple example shows that our minds are totally mesmerized by our senses, and they accordingly drive the mind. But to see the world as it is, Gaurav needs to be out of his mind as only then he can see the oneness of this world. The most incredible thing is that all this has always been happening under our noses, but for some reason, we behave as we live on a flat earth. If we really felt deeply how this whole phenomenon of life is happening, then being amazed, stunned and curious will not be an exaggeration.

He knows he is just scratching the surface of his mind, but he can already see that there are so many subtler processes and subtler laws that apply to our mind, similar to the laws of nature that cannot be changed. So, is it intelligent? Is it smart of us to live without understanding our mind and the structure of our mind? Or is it more intelligent to know the most sophisticated tool that nature has created?

Life is immense in every aspect and cannot be measured by our thoughts. It's infinite as our universe and our mind and body are incredible gifts of nature for us to experience this life. The human mind has already evolved and created so many amazing things over the centuries for human well being, but at the same time, the human mind is also responsible for all the atrocities caused to human beings, animals, and the planet. Only by understanding our mind at an individual level will there be a possibility of real transformation and change in this world.